CLAUDIA AND THE NEW GIRL

CLAUDIA AND THE NEW GIRL

Ann M. Martin

AN
APPLE
PAPERBACK

SCHOLASTIC INC.
New York Toronto London Auckland Sydney

This book is for the loyal readers
of The Baby-sitters Club *books.*

Cover art by Hodges Soileau

ISBN 0-590-25167-8

12 11 10 9 8 7 6   8 9/9 0/0

Printed in the U.S.A.   40

CHAPTER 1

I'd been watching this fly for ages. First it had landed on the back of Austin Bentley's head and crawled around on his hair for a full minute. Then it had flown to Dorianne Wallingford's right sneaker, but had had to move when Dorianne used her sneaker to scratch the back of her left leg. It tried Pete Black's pencil, but Pete flicked the pencil immediately and sent the fly on its way again.

I wondered whether the fly was a boy or a girl. I wondered whether flies have families. I wondered whether flies have family reunions and decided they didn't, because family reunions are almost always picnics, and at a flies' picnic, how could you tell the guest flies from the regular, uninvited flies who just want to land on the food for awhile? Then I wondered what it would be like to look out through those gigantic fly eyes, and whether flies would say "eyesight" or "flysight."

I wondered whether the fly found English class as thoroughly boring as I did. I'll say this about Mrs. Hall, our teacher. She at least *tries* to make the class interesting. For instance, most of the other English classes in our grade have to read *The Yearling* and *A Tree Grows in Brooklyn*. Mrs. Hall is doing something different with us — this big project on books that have won the Newbery Award. This gives us a pretty wide selection of books (and some of them are an awful lot shorter than *The Yearling*), but the thing is I just don't like to read. Except for Nancy Drew mysteries. They're fun. And I'm a pretty good sleuth.

Mrs. Hall was talking about *From the Mixed-up Files of Mrs. Basil E. Frankweiler* and *The Westing Game*. Okay, I'll admit it. I hadn't gotten around to reading either one, even though there is a character in *Mixed-up Files* with my name — Claudia. In fact, the only Newbery Award-winner I had read so far was this one called *Sarah, Plain and Tall*. That was because it was just fifty-eight pages long.

"Claudia?" said Mrs. Hall.

"Yes?" (Was she just trying to get my attention or had she asked me some question?)

"Can you help us out here?" (I guess she'd asked a question.) I could feel the blood rising to my face. I looked down at my notebook in which I'd been doodling pictures of some of the kids I baby-sit for. "Um, with what?" I replied.

Mrs. Hall sighed. "Claudia Kishi." (This was not a good sign. Mrs. Hall hardly ever uses our last names.) "Would you *please* pay attention?"

I nodded. "Yes," I managed to reply.

Mrs. Hall shook her head sadly. I wanted to add, "Sorry for ruining your day," because that's just what she looked like — a person whose day had been ruined. By *me!* I felt kind of powerful, although I wasn't proud of it. Imagine being able to ruin a grown-up's entire day single-handedly.

Mrs. Hall took my boredom pretty hard. "Class, please close your books and take out a fresh piece of paper. I want to give you a spelling check." ("Check" is Mrs. Hall's term for "surprise quiz.")

The class groaned. A few kids directed murderous glances at me, as if this whole thing were my fault. Well, I bet I hadn't been the only one watching that fly and doodling in my notebook.

"The words," Mrs. Hall went on, "will be taken from chapters seven and eight of *Mixed-up Files*, which you should have read last night."

"Should have" is right, I thought.

"The first word," Mrs. Hall said, "is 'pha-raoh.' "

I waited for her to use it in a sentence (not that it would do me any good). Mrs. Hall always uses spelling words in sentences, and she pronounces the sentences very carefully, with lots of emphasis.

"The *chil*dren are *stu*dying a *fa*mous E*gyp*tian *pha-raoh*."

Ah-ha! I thought. Mrs. Hall was giving us a hidden clue. She used "famous" and "pha-raoh" in the same sentence. They must begin with the same letter. Now, I'm a terrible speller, but I do know that "famous" begins with an "f." Very slowly, I printed "f-a-r-o" on my paper. Then, thoughtfully, I erased the "o" and added another "r." At the last moment, I tacked a "w" onto the end. That looked pretty good. Farrow. I was proud of myself for thinking to add one of those killer silent letters to the word. Who invented them, anyway? They're such a waste.

" 'Institute,' " Mrs. Hall went on.

I barely heard her. Outside the window, our varsity cheerleaders were practicing for our upcoming game against Stamford Junior High. They were really good. I wished I could do a split. Then I remembered what I was supposed

4

to be doing, and scribbled "instatute" on my paper. Not a moment too soon.

" 'Quarterly.' "

Before Mrs. Hall could use "quarterly" in one of her emphatic sentences, the door to our classroom opened. Every single head, including Mrs. Hall's, swiveled toward it. When we saw Ms. Downey, the school secretary, standing there, we grew really interested. The secretary only comes to a classroom for something major, otherwise the principal sends a student messenger.

Mrs. Hall crossed the room to Ms. Downey, and the two of them put their heads together and whispered for a moment. I hate when grown-ups do that. Then they pulled apart, and Ms. Downey stepped back and showed someone else into the room. Mrs. Hall greeted her warmly. "Hello, Ashley," she said, smiling. "We're happy to have you."

Then Ms. Downey handed Mrs. Hall some papers and left.

I was breathless. A new girl. We had a new girl in our class! I always think new kids, especially the ones who transfer in the middle of the school year — the middle of the *day*, for heaven's sake — are pretty interesting.

But this one (what had Mrs. Hall called her?) was more interesting than most. It was her clothes that first attracted my attention. They reminded me of something. What was it? Oh, yes. On television not long ago, I'd seen this bizarre movie called *Woodstock*. It was about a gigantic outdoor rock concert that took place ages ago, like in the sixties, and all the young people who attended it were what my parents call hippies. You know — they wore tons of beaded or silver jewelry and funny long skirts or bell-bottom jeans. The men pierced their ears and wore their hair in ponytails and the women looked like gypsies. (Only my mom said they were "bohemian." I think it means the same thing.)

Well, this girl, this Ashford or whatever her name was, looked like a hippie. She was wearing a very pretty pink flowered skirt that was full and so long it touched the tops of her shoes — which I soon realized were not shoes, but sort of hiking boots. Her blouse, loose and lacy, was embroidered with pink flowers, and both her wrists were loaded with silver bangle bracelets. Her hair, which was almost as long as my friend Dawn's and was dirty blonde, was pulled into a fat braid (which, I might add, was not held in place with a rubber band or anything; it just sort of trailed to an end). But the amazing thing was that because her hair was pulled back, you could see her ears.

And she had *three pierced earrings* in *each* ear. They were all silver and all dangly, but none matched.

Wow. Was she ever lucky. My parents would never let me have *six* holes.

Boy, would I have something to tell the other members of the Baby-sitters Club that afternoon.

The girl, looking fragile and delicate, faced my classmates and me.

"Class," said Mrs. Hall, "this is Ashley Wyeth. She's just moved to Stoneybrook and will be joining us for English. I hope you'll make her feel at home."

Mrs. Hall directed Ashley to the one empty desk in the room, which happened to be right next to mine. My heart leapt. Someone new, someone different. English class had suddenly become much more interesting.

The spelling check continued and I tried to pay attention, but my eyes kept drifting to Ashley Wyeth. Not to her paper. She probably hadn't read *From the Mixed-up Files of Mrs. Basil E. Frankweiler*, and anyway I wouldn't cheat. No, I was just looking at Ashley. I couldn't get over the way she was dressed . . . or her six earrings.

Then there was the matter of her last name. Wyeth. I wondered if that was Wyeth as in

Andrew Wyeth, the famous painter. I may not be a wonderful student, but I'm a pretty good artist, and I hoped that maybe I could grow up to be as good an artist as Andrew Wyeth. Even half as good would be okay with me.

On my fourth peek at Ashley, just after I'd spelled out m-e-d-i-c-l-e, I caught her peeking back at me. We both looked quickly at our papers. Then I looked a fifth time. Ashley was looking, too. I smiled at her. But she didn't smile back.

When the spelling check was over, we passed our papers forward and Mrs. Hall collected them in a tidy pile.

"Ashley," she said, after she'd stuck the papers in a folder on her desk, "we're discussing two books right now — *The Westing Game* and *From the Mixed-up Files of Mrs. Basil E. Frankweiler.* Have you read either of them?"

"Yes, I have," replied Ashley.

"Which one, dear?"

"Both of them."

Mrs. Hall raised her eyebrows.

"We studied the Newbery Award-winners in my old school last year," she said seriously.

"Mm-hmm." Mrs. Hall looked slightly disappointed. "And have you read *The Yearling?* Or *A Tree Grows in Brooklyn?*" I could tell she was thinking of transferring Ashley to one of the other English classes.

Ashley nodded. "I read them over the summer. But I don't mind doing the Newbery books again. I mean, we didn't read *all* of them. There are too many. Maybe I could do a special project on some of the older ones. The ones from the nineteen-thirties, if that's okay."

Mrs. Hall looked impressed. I was pretty impressed myself. What kind of kid got away with suggesting work to a teacher?

When class was over, Ashley and I looked at each other again. Then Ashley said quietly, "Um, hi. Do you know where room two-sixteen is?" It sounded as if it were killing her to have to talk to me. She certainly wasn't the friendliest person I'd ever met.

"Sure," I answered. "It's on the way to my math class. I'll take you."

"Oh, okay. . . . Thanks."

Ashley and I edged into the crowded hallway and headed for a staircase.

"My name's Claudia," I told her. "Claudia Kishi. Um, I was wondering. I know this sounds funny, but are you related to Andrew Wyeth?"

"No," replied Ashley. She paused, as if

deciding whether to say anything else. Then she added, "I wish I were, though."

So she knew who I meant!

"Boy, so do I," I told her.

"Do you like his work?" asked Ashley. She glanced at me, then quickly looked away.

"*Like* it? I love it! I take all kinds of art classes. I want to be a painter some day. Or a sculptress. Or maybe a potter."

"You do?" said Ashley. "So do I. I mean, I want to be a sculptress."

She was going to say something more then, but the warning bell rang and we had to duck into our classrooms. Before I did, though, I glanced once more at Ashley's retreating figure. I knew that somebody very . . . different had walked into my life.

CHAPTER 2

I didn't see Ashley again that day, but no wonder. There were only two periods left, and I had a remedial math class (that's math for kids who have a tough time with it) and a help session in the Resource Room. No way a smart kid like Ashley would have either remedial math or time in the Resource Room.

I was a little disappointed at not seeing Ashley again, but I had a meeting of the Baby-sitters Club to go to that afternoon, and I always look forward to meetings. Remember I mentioned my friend Dawn? Dawn Schafer is the one whose hair is longer and blonder than Ashley's. Well, she's in the club, too, and so are my other friends, Kristy Thomas, Mary Anne Spier, and Stacey McGill. The club is really fun. We meet three times a week, and people here in Stoneybrook, Connecticut, call us when they need baby-sitters. We get lots of jobs and I earn lots of money, which is im-

11

portant, because I need it to buy art supplies and makeup and jewelry and stuff.

As you can probably see, the club is really a little business. It's a year old now, and we run it very professionally. Here's how it works: we meet in my room on Monday, Wednesday, and Friday afternoons from five-thirty till six. (We use my room because I have my own private phone and phone number. For that reason, I get to be vice-president of the club.) Our clients know they can call us at our meeting times. Then they tell us when they need sitters and one of us signs up for each job. With five of us here, our clients almost always find a sitter with just one phone call, and they really like that. You're probably wondering what happens if two or three of us are able to take the same job. Who gets it? Well, luckily, we're busy enough so that doesn't happen very often. When it does, we're pretty nice about saying things like, "Well, I've got two other jobs signed up that week. You take it, Stacey," or, "David Michael is your little brother, Kristy. You take the job."

Mary Anne, our club secretary, keeps track of all our jobs in the appointment pages of our club record book. In fact, she's responsible for the whole record book (except for the account of how much money we earn). The record

12

book is where we note the addresses and phone numbers of our clients, information on the kids, our job appointments, and other commitments, like art classes.

Stacey's our treasurer, so she keeps track of the money we earn, as well as the money in our treasury, which comes from the dues we pay each week. Our dues money goes for club expenses. For instance, we pay Kristy's big brother Charlie to drive her to and from each meeting. This is only fair, since Kristy, our president, started the club but had to move out of our neighborhood over the summer. We also use the treasury money to buy coloring books and stuff for the Kid-Kits. (Kid-Kits are something Kristy thought up. They're cardboard cartons filled with our old books, games, and toys, plus activity books and crayons and other things we buy, which we sometimes take with us when we go on a baby-sitting job. Whenever one of us brings a Kid-Kit, we're a huge hit.)

Here are some other things you should know about the club: Dawn is our alternate officer, which means she's like a substitute teacher. She can take over the job of any other member who has to miss a meeting. We also have two associate members, Logan Bruno and Shannon Kilbourne. They're sitters we can call on in a pinch if a job comes in that none of us can take. (Luckily, that doesn't happen very often.) Last thing — aside from the club record book, we keep a notebook. Kristy insists on this. In the notebook, we write up every single job we go on, and then we're responsible for reading the other entries about once a week. That way, we know what went on when our friends were sitting, which is often very helpful. (But — do you want my honest opinion? Reading that notebook every week can be a total bore.)

When school was over on the day I met Ashley Wyeth, I ran right home and did what was left of my homework (a lot of it had gotten done in the Resource Room), and then I took a look at *Mixed-up Files*. It really was time I read it, especially if Mrs. Hall was going to give us "checks" on it every now and then.

I read until 5:15. The story wasn't bad. After all, there was a girl named Claudia in it. Furthermore, this Claudia felt that she was a victim of injustice. When I looked up "injustice" and found out what it meant, I was pretty interested. I often think things in my life are unjust, particularly where school or my genius sister Janine is concerned.

At 5:15, I went downstairs to find my grandmother Mimi and wait for the members of the Baby-sitters Club to come over.

Mimi was in the kitchen, starting supper. She had a stroke last summer but is much better now except for two things. She can only use her left hand (she used to be right-handed), and she still has a little trouble with her speech — but not much, considering that Japanese, not English, is her native language. Anyway, she likes to feel useful, so she insists on starting dinner every weekday afternoon while my parents are at work, and doing whatever housework she can manage.

"Ah. Hello, my Claudia," Mimi greeted me when I entered the kitchen. "You have been study hard?"

"I guess so," I replied. "I'm reading this book. Some of the words are pretty big, but I like it. It's funny."

"How about having special tea?" asked Mimi.

"Oh, I can't. I mean, I don't have time. We have a club meeting. Everyone'll be here in about ten minutes."

"Ah. Yes. I see." (That's what Mimi always says these days when she wants to say something *else*, but the right words won't come.)

"Mimi," I began, pulling a cutting board toward me and starting to peel carrots for the salad, "there's a new girl in school. She's in my English class. Her name is Ashley Wyeth, and she likes art just like I do. We only talked

15

for a couple of minutes today, but I think maybe we're going to be friends. Isn't that funny?"

"It happens that way sometimes. Happen when I meet your grandfather. In one second I know . . . knew . . . we would fall in love, be married, have children."

"Really?" I said. I was awed. What a second that must have been. I guess you *need* those seconds to make up for all the dull ones when you're just watching flies land on people's heads.

The doorbell rang then and I ran to answer it. It was probably Kristy. She often arrives either early or late since she's at the mercy of Charlie's schedule.

Sure enough, it was Kristy. She let herself in even before I'd answered the door.

"Hi, Claudia!" she cried. She looked like she was in a really good mood, but I wished for the thirty-nine thousandth time that she'd do something about her clothes and hair. Kristy is really cute, but she never bothers to make herself look special. All fall she's been wearing the same kind of outfit — jeans, a turtleneck, a sweater, and sneakers. And she hasn't been doing a thing to her long (well, longish) brown hair except brushing it. Here's an example of one of the big differences between Kristy and me. I was wearing a very short pink cotton dress, white tights, and black ballet slippers. I had swept all of my hair way over to one side, where it was held in place with a piece of pink cloth that matched the dress. Only one ear showed, and in it I had put my big palm tree earring. (Kristy was not wearing any jewelry.)

We are so different, it is amazing.

Dawn, Mary Anne, and Stacey arrived a few minutes later. Actually, as you might guess, we are *all* different — but some of us are more different than others. Stacey is kind of like me. She wears trendy clothes and is always getting her hair styled or permed or something, but she's not as outrageous as I can be. I did notice that day, though, that she had painted her fingernails yellow and then put black polka dots all over them.

Mary Anne, who is quiet and shy, dresses more like Kristy (who's a loudmouth). But Mary Anne is beginning to pay some attention to what she wears. Dawn falls in between Stacey and me, and Kristy and Mary Anne. She's just an individual. She's originally from California and tends to dress casually, but with flair.

The five of us went upstairs to my room and closed the door. I found a bag of Doritos in my stash of junk food and passed it around, while Kristy took her seat in my director's chair and Mary Anne opened the record book so she'd be ready with our appointment calendar when the first call came in.

While we ate the Doritos and waited for the phone to ring, I said, "Did any of you see that new girl? Ashley Wyeth?"

The others shook their heads. But nobody made any snide comments about new girls. That's because Stacey and Dawn were both new girls themselves not too far back. (Stacey's from New York City. She moved to Stoneybrook about a year ago, which was about six months before Dawn moved here from California.)

Ring, ring! We all leapt for the phone. That usually happens with the first call of the meeting. Kristy got it, though.

"Hello, Baby-sitters Club," she said in her most adult voice. "Hi, Mrs. Rodowsky. . . . Thursday? That's short notice, but I'll check and call you right back, okay? 'Bye."

"Mrs. Rodowsky?" I said, groaning, as Kristy hung up the phone. The Rodowskys have three boys, and one of them, Jackie, is completely accident-prone. The only thing that ever happens when you sit at the Rodowskys' is that Jackie falls off things, on things, or into things. Sometimes he gets caught in things or breaks things or loses things. He's a nice little kid, but *sheesh.*

Mary Anne began to giggle. "Hey, guess what, Claud?" she said. "You're the only one who's free that day."

"Oh, no!" I clapped my hand to my forehead as Kristy picked up the phone to call Mrs. Rodowsky back. But I didn't mind as much as I let on. I've sat for Jackie and his brothers a few times now, and Jackie's beginning to grow on me.

The meeting continued. Calls came in, we got jobs. It was your average meeting. Pretty uneventful.

I loved every second of it.

The Baby-sitters Club is very important to me. It's almost as important to me as art is. I don't know what I'd do without the club — or my friends.

CHAPTER 3

All that night and all the next morning on my way to school, I looked forward to seeing Ashley Wyeth again. Would she be in any of my other classes? What was her morning schedule? But I didn't see her until English class, not even at lunchtime, although she must have been in the cafeteria since everyone in my grade eats at the same time.

In English, I smiled at her and she smiled back, but when the bell rang at the end of class, Mrs. Hall asked to see me privately, so I missed walking upstairs with Ashley. (By the way, I wasn't in any trouble. Mrs. Hall just wanted to assign me some grammar stuff to work on in the Resource Room.) I couldn't believe I had completely missed Ashley. Oh, well. Maybe the next day.

That afternoon, I went to one of my art classes. I'm taking two kinds of classes right now. One is this general art class where we get to work in all different media. (That means we get to sculpt, draw, sketch, and paint in acrylics, watercolors, and oils.) We're working on sculpture now. I like it, but it's hard. I'm better at painting and drawing. On the weekends I take a pottery class. Pottery is my new love. Over the summer my family went to this mountain resort where you could swim, ride horses, go on hikes, and take art classes. (It was sort of like camp, except it was for adults, too.) Anyway, I went to some pottery classes and *loved* throwing pots, so Mom and Dad signed me up for a Saturday class in Stoneybrook.

Since the Stoneybrook Arts Center isn't far from Stoneybrook Middle School, I got to my class a little early that day. I was the second person there. (I'd even beaten the teacher.) I set up the piece I was working on in class and was about to make a little change on one part when someone tapped me on the shoulder.

I turned around.

"Ashley!" I exclaimed.

There she was. She was wearing a puffy white blouse, a blue-jean jacket, a long blue-jean skirt, and those hiking boots again. Beaded bracelets circled both wrists, and she'd tied a strip of faded denim around her head, like an Indian headband. Since her hair was loose that day, I couldn't get a good look at her ears. I wanted to see if she was wearing six earrings again.

"Hi, Claudia," she said, fixing her serious gaze on me. "I can't believe you're in this class."

"You're joining it?" I cried, even though it was obvious that she was.

Ashley nodded. "I took lots of art classes in Chicago. This was the only one we could find here, though. Is it a good class?"

"It's great. You should see all the stuff we're doing."

"What's the teacher like?"

"Ms. Baehr? She's nice. Really, you know, encouraging."

"Where did she study?" Ashley wanted to know. "Has she exhibited any of her work?"

"Huh?" I replied brightly.

"What's her background? Is she qualified?"

I could feel my cheeks burning. Of course Ms. Baehr was qualified. She was the teacher. If she weren't qualified, she couldn't teach . . . could she? "I — I don't know," I stammered, but Ashley was already off on another subject. She eyed my sculpture, which was of a hand. Just a hand. If you think it's easy to sculpt (or draw) a realistic hand, try it sometime.

"Hey, Claudia, that's terrific," said Ashley.

"It's beautiful." She walked all around the hand, looking at it from different angles.

"Thanks," I said. "It's just an exercise piece, though. I'm practicing on it, learning things."

"Well, it's still terrific. What else have you done?"

I noticed that Ashley was carrying a portfolio under one arm. "Do you want to see my portfolio?" I asked her shyly. I always feel like I'm bragging when I offer to let someone look through my portfolio, even though I'm not sure my work is all that good. Lots of people say it is, but I usually think, What do they know?

"Sure," replied Ashley.

"Well . . . okay," I said uncertainly. Our portfolios are stored on shelves that line the back wall of the room. I retrieved mine, laid it on the worktable next to my sculpture, and opened it for Ashley.

Very slowly, Ashley looked at every sketch and drawing that I'd saved in the portfolio. She turned them over one by one and studied each before going on to the next. I stood across from her, watching her face for a reaction. I felt as nervous as if I were waiting for a teacher to tell me whether I'd passed into the next grade.

When Ashley was finished, she closed the

portfolio and regarded me gravely with china-blue eyes. "You are really talented," she said. "I hope you know that."

I let out a sigh of relief. "Oh, thanks," I replied. "I'm glad you liked everything." Since art is one of the few things I think I'm any good at, I just die if people *don't* like my work. I hesitated. "Could I look at your portfolio?" I asked her. "Would you mind?"

"Oh, no. I wouldn't mind." Ashley slid her portfolio across the table to me.

I opened it, wondering what kind of artist Ashley was. You can tell a lot from a person's portfolio. I always look at the subjects that the person has chosen to draw or paint, and the pieces that she's decided to save in the portfolio. That kind of thing. It's psychological, I guess.

Ashley's first drawing nearly made me gasp. It drove all thoughts of psychology right out of my head. I had never seen a more realistic portrait in my life. It looked like a photograph.

I'm sure my eyes were bugging out in a really undignified way.

"Whoa," I whispered. "Amazing."

Ashley waved her hand at it. "That's not really anything," she said. "It's old. But this *next* one . . ."

I turned to the next piece in the portfolio. It was a watercolor. I wasn't sure what it was a watercolor *of*, but I knew it was very, very good.

"*That* is innovation," Ashley told me.

I glanced at her to see if she was kidding, but she looked as grave and serious as always.

The rest of Ashley's portfolio was as amazing as the beginning. When I finally closed the folder, my heart was pounding. "How long have you been taking art lessons?" I asked.

"Oh, forever," Ashley replied. "Since I was four or five."

"Wow. Where did you take lessons? Anywhere special?"

"Do you know the Keyes Art Society? It's in Chicago. That's where I used to live."

"You studied at *Keyes?!*" I could barely contain my excitement.

Ashley nodded.

"Wow. But how'd you get in? Only a few kids are chosen to study there." Keyes was famous among art students. I once asked my parents if I could try to get in for the summer session, but they said it was too far way and *much* too expensive.

"I was just chosen," Ashley said modestly. "When I was eight." She looked uncertainly around our little room in the Stoneybrook Arts Center. "I hope this school is good. And I hope Ms. Baehr is as good as Mr. Simmons. Mr. Simmons was my old teacher."

"Oh, I'm sure it's all . . . fine," I lied. "Wow, did you really like my portfolio?"

"Are you kidding? It's fantastic. If you lived in Chicago you could go to Keyes."

"Wow. . . ." I felt as if the floor were melting away under my feet. A person who had gone to *Keyes* thought *my* work was good. I hoped I was impressing Ashley as much as she was impressing me.

A bunch of kids had arrived by then and I introduced Ashley to them. I thought it was a good way for her to get to know some other kids in Stoneybrook. But Ashley didn't seem very interested in the other students. I noticed that she always looked at a kid's sculpture (not at the actual kid) while I was making introductions. Then she'd just kind of nod, and we'd go on to the next person. The only person she looked at for a moment was Fiona McRae, the second best student in the class. (I'm the first. At least, I was the first until Ashley arrived.) Ashley looked appreciatively from Fiona's sculpture of a stag to Fiona and back to the stag before we moved on. Then I showed Ashley where our supplies were stored, and *then*, just as Ashley was sitting down next to me, Ms. Baehr entered the room.

Ashley got to her feet, looking both nervous and hopeful, and I introduced her to our teacher.

Ms. Baehr was apparently expecting Ashley and seemed just as impressed that Ashley had studied at Keyes as I had been. She looked through Ashley's portfolio, raising her eyebrows, murmuring to herself. I knew I should feel jealous, but I didn't. After all, Ashley had studied at Keyes and she'd said *I* was really talented. She ought to know. Furthermore, she'd chosen me (out of all the kids in the class) to be her friend. She'd barely looked at the other kids, and the only people she'd talked to were Ms. Baehr and me.

I was so wound up, I thought I couldn't stand another ounce of excitement.

And just as I was thinking that, Ms. Baehr finished talking to Ashley, went to the front of the room, and said, "I have an announcement to make. A new art gallery will be opening in Stoneybrook, and in honor of the opening, the owners have planned a sculpture contest for the students at the Arts Center. I'd like all of you to think about entering. You can start a new piece for the show or finish one of the pieces you're working on now. Even if you

27

don't win, your entry will be exhibited at the gallery the week it opens. I think it would be a good experience for all of you."

Ashley turned to me excitedly. "A show!" she whispered. "Oh, we *have* to enter!"

"Is there a prize?" Fiona McRae wanted to know.

"First prize is two hundred and fifty dollars," replied Ms. Baehr.

Wow! What I could buy with two hundred and fifty dollars! It was mind-boggling.

"When's the show? I mean, what's the deadline for entering?" asked John Steiner.

"Four weeks from today."

Only four weeks. My face fell. I could kiss the prize money good-bye. No way could I have something good enough to enter in a month. My hand was a practice piece, not a show piece. At home, I was working on two sculptures — one of Mimi (my favorite subject) and one of Mary Anne's kitten, Tigger. The Mimi sculpture was too personal to enter, and Tigger wasn't the right kind of thing for a show. No, if I were going to enter, I'd have to start from scratch. And a month wasn't enough time to start *and* finish a piece, take my pottery course, keep up in school, and baby-sit.

"I can't enter," I told Ashley later, when class had begun.

Ashley looked up from the lump of clay before her. "Why not?"

I explained my reasons.

"You have to enter," said Ashley. "It would be a sin not to. You shouldn't waste your talent. I could help you," she went on. "I bet I could teach you lots of things. Show you ways to branch out. And I only spend time on people with talent."

"I can't enter," I said simply.

"Well, I'm going to. If it's all I do for the next four weeks, I'm going to create a piece worth entering. And I think you should, too. Remember. I'll help you."

"We-ell," I said. "I'll see."

Ashley smiled. "I thought you'd change your mind," she said.

CHAPTER 4

"Oh, no! Look out!" I cried.

THUD! Crunch, crunch.

"Oops," said Jackie Rodowsky.

I buried my face in my hands. I was hoping that maybe when I opened my eyes the Rice Krispies would have disappeared from the kitchen floor. But no, when I took my hands away, the linoleum was still covered with a crunchy carpet of cereal, and Jackie was still sitting in the middle of the mess with the overturned box in his hands.

It was Thursday, and my ordeal with the Rodowskys had only just begun. After his mother had left, the very first words out of Jackie's mouth had been, "I'm hungry. Let's make a snack." The next thing I knew I was up to my ankles in Rice Krispies.

I glanced at the kitchen table, where nine-year-old Shea and four-year-old Archie were sitting. (Can you imagine naming a helpless

30

little baby Archibald?) Shea and Archie were never any trouble. Well, not usually. They might *look* exactly like Jackie, but that red-haired, freckle-faced seven-year-old was the only walking disaster in the Rodowsky house.

"Well, let's clean up," I said with a sigh. I meant for Jackie and me to clean up, but Shea and Archie leaped out of their chairs, disappeared for a moment, and returned with a dustpan and brush, and a mini vacuum cleaner. They know everything there is to know about cleaning. Life with Jackie has done that to them.

Archie held the dustpan, Shea swept the cereal into it, and I followed them around, vacuuming up Rice Krispie dust.

Jackie watched from the sidelines. "What can I do?" he asked.

"Stand still," I replied.

But for Jackie, that was much, much easier said than done.

I concentrated on making sure that Shea and Archie and I left no traces of cereal on the floor. Then I helpfully added "Rice Krispys" to Mrs. Rodowsky's grocery list, which was fastened to the refrigerator with a magnet.

I was just finishing when I heard Shea speak the dreaded words: "Where's Jackie?"

"Uh-oh," I said. "Shea, you and Archie look

31

upstairs. I'll look down here and in the rec room."

The boys tore upstairs while I dashed into the living room and then the dining room. No Jackie and no signs of him, either — everything was intact and unstained. I leaned down into the rec room. "Jackie?" I called.

No answer.

Then I heard Shea's voice. "Um, Claudia? Can you come here?"

I ran upstairs and found Shea and Archie standing outside the bathroom. The door to the bathroom was closed.

"Is Jackie in there?" I asked.

"Yes," answered Shea. "And the door's locked."

"Hey, Jackie!" I yelled. "Unlock the door! You know how to do that, don't you?"

"Yeah!" he replied. "Only I can't."

"How come?"

"I'm stuck in the bathtub."

"How can you be stuck in the bathtub?"

"My hand's down the drain. I can't get it out."

Archie tugged at the hem of my shirt. "He was trying to get his Blasto-Plane out. It gurgled right down the drain last night."

"Oh, for heaven's sake," I said, clapping my

hand to my forehead. "All right. Shea, where's the key to the bathroom?"

Shea shrugged.

"You don't *know?*" I exclaimed. Us baby-sitters think to ask parents a lot of questions, such as whether any of the children has food allergies and where the first-aid kit is, but I'd never bothered to ask about the key to the bathroom.

Shea looked at me, teary-eyed. "I'm sorry," he said.

"Oh, Shea. No, *I'm* sorry. I didn't mean to sound angry. It's just that I don't know how to help Jackie."

"I do," said Shea, brightening.

"You do?"

"Yeah. It's simple. Go in through the window."

"But Shea, we're upstairs," I reminded him.

"I know. All you do is get on the doghouse roof, then get on the toolshed roof, then get on the porch roof and you can open the bathroom window from there. Want me to do it?"

"No, thanks. I better be the one," I said grimly. "I hope the bathroom window isn't locked, too."

Five minutes later, I was standing on top of

the doghouse. Archie and Bo (the dog) were watching me. Shea was inside so he could talk to Jackie. As I struggled to hoist myself onto the toolshed, I thanked my lucky stars I was wearing blue jeans, and decided to wear jeans to the Rodowskys' from then on.

"Yea!" cried Archie as I walked unsteadily across the toolshed roof and began the last leg of my trip.

When at last I was standing by the bathroom window, I prayed silently, Please let it be open.

It was. "Thank you," I said as I crawled into the bathroom.

"For what?" asked Jackie.

"I didn't mean you," I told him.

I unlocked the bathroom door. Shea was still standing patiently in the hallway. Now what? I thought, eyeing Jackie with his hand down the drain. All at once I had an idea. It was a good idea, and it also made me appreciate the Baby-sitters Club Notebook a whole lot more than I ever had. I'd just remembered reading about how Mary Anne and Logan Bruno had once gotten Jackie's hand out of a mayonnaise jar.

"Shea," I said, "could you run into the kitchen and get me some margarine? Oh, and also call Archie inside."

"Sure," replied Shea. In a moment he returned with Archie and a tub of margarine.

I rubbed a healthy, greasy amount around Jackie's hand and the edge of the drain. "Now pull your hand up very slowly," I instructed him.

He did, and after adding a few more glops of margarine, his hand was free.

"Whew," I said.

"Whew," said Jackie.

"Whew," said Shea and Archie.

"Why don't we go outside?" I suggested. Somehow, the Rodowskys' yard seemed much safer than the inside of their house.

"Okay," agreed the boys. So as soon as we'd cleaned the margarine off Jackie, we went into the front yard. The front yard was closer to the street, but there wasn't much room to play in the backyard, what with Bo's house and the toolshed and all.

"What do you want to play?" I asked the boys. They couldn't agree on anything, so I said, "Do you know Red Light, Green Light?"

Three red heads shook slowly from side to side.

"Okay, it's easy," I told them. "You guys stand here." I lined them up on one side of the yard. Then I ran to the other side. "I'm the policeman. When I turn around and close my eyes, I'll say, 'Green light.' Then you start sneaking up on me. But don't go too fast. Because when I say, 'Red light,' I'm going to turn around again and open my eyes. And anyone I see moving has to go back to the beginning. The first one to sneak all the way over here and tag me is the winner and gets to be the new policeman. Got it?"

"Got it," said Shea.

"Got it," said Jackie.

"Got what?" asked Archie.

"Never mind," I said. "Let's start the game and see what happens. If you don't understand the rules, stop and tell me, okay?"

Archie nodded.

"Now remember," I went on. "I'm the policeman, so you have to do what I say." I turned my back and closed my eyes. "Green light!" I shouted.

I heard rustlings as the boys snuck toward me.

"Red light!" I spun toward them as I opened my eyes. Shea and Archie, both about a third of the way across the yard, were standing stock-still in running position, as if they'd been on a videotape and someone had pushed the pause button on the VCR. But Jackie, who was slightly ahead of them, was still moving. When he tried to freeze, he lost his balance and fell over. "Okay, back to start," I told him.

Grumbling, Jackie took his time returning to the opposite side of the yard. When he was ready, I closed my eyes and called, "Green light!" again. Almost immediately, I felt a tap on my shoulder. "Winner!" I announced in surprise. Who had reached me so quickly? I opened my eyes.

Ashley Wyeth was at my side.

"Ashley!" I exclaimed.

The three Rodowsky boys, who didn't know whether to stop or go, all lost their balance and toppled to the ground.

I giggled, but Ashley was looking at me strangely.

"What are you doing?" she asked.

"Baby-sitting," I replied. "We're playing Red Light, Green Light. What are *you* doing? I mean, what are you doing *here?*"

"I live next door." Ashley pointed to the house to the right of the Rodowskys'.

The Rodowsky boys had recovered their balance and abandoned the game. They crowded around Ashley. I guess they'd never seen anyone wearing a long petticoat and workboots. Not anyone from the twentieth century, anyway.

"Why do you have to baby-sit?" Ashley asked me.

(The boys looked somewhat hurt.)

"I don't *have* to," I replied. "This is my job. I love sitting." I told her about the Baby-sitters Club and how it works and the kids we sit for.

"What do you do in your spare time?" I asked Ashley.

"I paint. Or sculpt," she replied.

"I mean, what do you and your friends do? Well, what did you guys do in Chicago?"

"Just . . . just my artwork. That's really all that's important to me. I had one friend, another girl from Keyes. Sometimes we painted together. The only way to develop your talent is to devote time to it, you know."

I listened to Ashley with interest. She must know what she was talking about, being from Keyes and all. Maybe, I thought, I should set aside one afternoon a week just for my art. No distractions, no interruptions. I bet Ashley did that — and more.

"The baby-sitting club must take up a lot of your time," said Ashley.

"It does," I answered proudly. "The club's doing really well."

38

"But when do you have time for your sculpting?"

"Whenever I make time," I replied. Was Ashley saying I wasn't serious enough about my art?

Ashley frowned slightly at Archie, who had wrapped his arms around my legs and was blowing raspberries on my blue jeans. Suddenly I felt embarrassed and sort of . . . babyish. I unwound Archie and stepped away from him.

"I," I said, "spend plenty of time on my art. In fact, I've decided I have enough time to enter something in the sculpture show."

Ashley smiled. "Good," she said. Then she started to walk away.

"Hey, don't you want to stay for awhile?" I asked her.

"Well, I do. I mean, I'd like to talk. But — " (she paused, eyeing the Rodowskys as if they were ants at a picnic) " — not right now."

And then she left.

I thought about Ashley for most of the rest of the afternoon. She seemed so grown-up. She was serious and she set goals for herself and then went right ahead and worked toward them. That was how I wanted to be — serious and grown-up, just like Ashley. As I rode my bike home from the Rodowskys' that day, I decided two things: I would let Ashley help me with my sculpture, since she had offered. And I would not let her see me play any more stupid outdoor games when I sat at the Rodowskys'.

CHAPTER 5

One of the very nicest things about the Baby-sitters Club is how it has made good friends out of the five members. A year ago, we were all split up. Mary Anne and Kristy, because they were a little immature and were already best friends anyway, always stuck together. And when Stacey moved to town, she and I were so much alike (and so different from Kristy and Mary Anne) that we became best friends immediately. The four of us hardly ever hung around together, except at meetings. We even ate lunch with different groups of friends. Then Dawn moved to Stoneybrook. She became Mary Anne's friend first, but once she joined the club, she was sort of friends with all of us and would go back and forth between our crowds in the cafeteria.

This year is different, though. Right off the bat, the five of us club members started eating together and going places together and generally being a group (even though we've got non-club friends). It's just expected that when that bell rings before lunch period, we'll all run to the cafeteria, and the first one down there will save our favorite table.

So when Ashley Wyeth caught up with me in the hallway on my way to the cafeteria the day after I'd sat at the Rodowskys' and said, "Let's eat lunch together, Claudia," I wasn't sure how to answer her. I didn't want to desert my friends.

Finally I said, "Do you want to sit with my friends and me? The members of the Baby-sitters Club always eat together."

Ashley thought that over. Then she said, "Let's sit by ourselves. You don't *always* sit with them, do you? Besides, what are you going to talk about? Baby-sitting?"

"Not necessarily," I replied. "We talk about lots of things, like boys and school dances and . . . and . . . stuff."

"Well, we need to discuss art," said Ashley.

"You and me?"

"Who else around here knows as much about sculpture as we do?"

I felt extremely flattered.

"We have an art show to enter," Ashley reminded me. "We have to figure out what the subjects of our sculptures are going to be. I'd like to help you, if you want help."

Did I want help from a person who'd studied at Keyes? I thought. Of course I did. "Oh, thanks. That'd be great," I told her. "But don't you mean *who* the subjects will be?"

Ashley smiled and shook her head.

Mystified, I pushed open the double doors at the back of the cafeteria.

Ashley headed toward a table by the windows that overlooked the playing fields, but I pulled her in the opposite direction. "I have to talk to my friends for a sec first," I told her. Then I paused. "Are you *sure* you don't want to sit with them?"

"I just don't think we'd get anything accomplished," Ashley replied. "Time is valuable — if you want to become a great artist."

"I guess so."

My heart began to pound. How would the club members react when one of us "defected"? It wasn't like I was sick or had to do makeup work in the Resource Room or something.

I led Ashley over to the Baby-sitters Club's table, where Kristy and Mary Anne were just settling down with trays. They'd bought the hot lunch, and as usual, Kristy was making comments about it. "*I* know what this looks like!'' she was exclaiming, indicating the pizza-burger. "It looks like . . . remember that squir-rel that got run over?"

Next to me, Ashley was turning green, so I said hastily, "Hi, you guys."

"Oh, hi!" said Mary Anne. She pulled a chair out for me. "Dawn and Stacey are buying milk. How come you're late?"

"Well," I replied, stalling for time. "It's . . . Do you guys know Ashley Wyeth? She's the new g — , I mean, she's new here. And she's in my art class. And, um, we're going to eat together today because we have to discuss something, this project," I said in a rush, not even giving anyone a chance to say hello.

Ashley slipped her arm possessively through mine.

"Oh," replied Kristy, shifting her eyes from Ashley and me to her tray. "Okay."

Mary Anne looked away, too, but didn't say anything.

Neither did Ashley. Finally I just said, "Well, um, see you guys later."

"Yeah. See you," said Kristy.

As Ashley and I made our way across the cafeteria, I began to feel angry. Why, I thought, shouldn't I have a new friend? Was there some law that said I had to eat lunch with Kristy, Mary Anne, Dawn, and Stacey every day? No,

44

of course not. They had no right to try to make me feel like I'd committed a federal crime or something.

"Hey," I said suddenly to Ashley as we set our books on an empty table. "Aren't we forgetting something?"

"What?" asked Ashley. She swept her hair over her shoulders, and I could see her ear-rings. Sure enough, six altogether. Two gold balls and a hoop in one ear. A seashell, a real feather, and a dangly flamingo in the other. Pretty cool.

"We forgot our lunches," I said, grinning.

Ashley broke into a smile. "Oh, yeah."

We left our things on the table and went through the lunch line. I never bring my lunch to school, but I refuse to buy the revolt-o hot lunch. I usually eat a sandwich instead. Ashley bought a yogurt and an apple. Health food. She and Dawn would probably get along great, since Dawn only eats stuff like fruit and granola and vegetables. It was too bad Ashley didn't seem to want to get to know my other friends.

When we returned to our table, Ashley said, "So, have you thought about what you want to sculpt?"

"No," I replied. This wasn't quite true. I had thought about it, but I'd been hoping Ashley would have some good ideas, since she was such an expert. "Do you have any ideas for your project?"

Ashley shook her head. "Well, I mean, there are plenty of possibilities. I just haven't narrowed them down. But I have a great idea. I read that there's a new exhibit opening at Kuller's Gallery."

Kuller's was the other gallery in Stoneybrook, the old one.

"I think it's a watercolor exhibit, but we ought to go check it out. I always get really inspired when I'm at a show."

"But we need ideas for sculptures," I said, "not paintings."

"You never know what might strike you, though."

I paused just long enough so that Ashley jumped back into the conversation with, "Oh, Claud, you *have* to go with me. Nobody else will appreciate the show the way you will."

I beamed. "Okay," I said. "I'll go. Just as long as I'm home by five-thirty. I've got a meeting of the Baby-sitters Club."

I didn't get home until 5:45. At five o'clock I'd started saying things to Ashley such as, "I better leave soon," and, "I really better go."

But every time I said something, Ashley would pull me over to another painting, saying,

"Just look at this one, Claud. You have to look at this one." She was so intense. I think she barely heard what I was saying.

I must admit, I got much more out of a show when Ashley was along than I did by myself. She made me look at paintings in different ways and see things in them that I wouldn't have noticed by myself. And she listened, really *listened*, to anything I had to say about the watercolors.

So I had a hard time leaving. I was just enjoying appreciating the art. I knew my other friends would never get so much out of an exhibit. They didn't enjoy art the way Ashley and I did.

At quarter of six when I finally ran into my bedroom, I found the club meeting in progress.

"You guys started without me!" I exclaimed accusingly.

"Hello yourself," said Kristy. "Of course we started without you. The phone began ringing. What did you expect? That we'd tell everyone to call back later — after Claudia got here? We weren't sure you were coming at all. Where were you?"

"Ashley and I went to an exhibit at Kuller's."

At the mention of Ashley's name, my friends exchanged glances.

"How come you didn't call to say you were

going to be late?" asked Kristy. "That's a club rule, you know."

"I was trying to get here," I said. "I ran the whole way home. I left the exhibit late. It was just . . . Ashley and I were having such a good time."

"*How* good a time?" spoke up Stacey, and I thought she looked a little pale. "As good a time as when you and I go to the mall?"

"Stace, I don't know," I said, forcing a laugh.

The phone rang, and we stopped our discussion to take a job. And then two more.

"What did I miss?" I finally dared to ask. "I mean, at the beginning of the meeting."

"Three calls," replied Kristy. "On the appointment pages, it looked like you were free for a couple of them, but we couldn't be sure. Stacey and Mary Anne took them instead."

I nodded. That was fair. And anyway, it was a rule. If you were going to be late to a meeting and didn't tell anyone about it first, you lost privileges. Still, I didn't like the way being left out felt.

Or the way Stacey was looking at me.

CHAPTER 6

Uh-oh, you guys. I had some trouble with Jeff today and it affected my baby-sitting, so I guess you should know about it. I was sitting at the Perkinses', and Myriah and Gabbie were being as good as gold. In fact, they were entertaining themselves really well. They had a messy project going, but it was in the bathroom, and Mrs. Perkins said it was all right because it would be easy to clean up. The three of us--Myriah and Gabbie and I -- were having a great time. Chewbacca wasn't even bothering us. And then the phone rang....

What you need to know about Dawn's younger brother Jeff is that ever since school started this year, he's been having problems. He's been saying he misses his father. See, the reason Dawn moved to Stoneybrook last January was that her parents had just gotten a divorce, and Stoneybrook is where Mrs. Schafer grew up. Her parents, Dawn's grandparents, still live here. So Mrs. Schafer moved Dawn and Jeff back to her hometown. Mr. Schafer stayed in California.

At first, things seemed okay. I mean, Dawn didn't like the cold Connecticut winter, but she made friends and joined our club, and Jeff made friends, and Mrs. Schafer found a job and even started dating. Then at the end of the summer, Dawn and Jeff flew back to California to visit their dad. Maybe Jeff got homesick or something. Who knows? Anyway, he's become a real handful. He's been saying he misses Mr. Schafer and that he doesn't want to live with Dawn and their mom anymore. And he's been getting into trouble in school. So that's what had been going on in Dawn's life at the time she took the job baby-sitting for Myriah and Gabbie Perkins.

When Dawn rang the Perkinses' bell it was

answered by the gallumphing feet of Chew-bacca, their big black Labrador retriever.

"Chewy! Chewy!" she could hear Mrs. Perkins saying. Then she heard a little scuffle. "Dawn?" Mrs. Perkins called.

"Yeah, it's me," Dawn replied.

"Let yourself in, okay? I'm going to put Chewy in the backyard."

"Okay!" Dawn opened the front door and stood listening. Apart from the sounds of Mrs. Perkins taking Chewbacca outside, she couldn't hear a thing. Where were Myriah and Gabbie? Usually they race to answer the door if one of us baby-sitters is coming over.

When Mrs. Perkins returned, she put a finger to her lips and whispered, "I want to show you something. Follow me."

Dawn followed Mrs. Perkins upstairs and into the girls' bathroom. Mrs. Perkins gestured for her to peek inside.

Dawn did. Seated on the (closed) toilet, she saw Gabbie, who's almost three, holding a mirror and carefully applying a streak of green eye shadow in a long line from one eye, across her nose, to her other eye. She looked like a cavewoman.

Myriah, who's six, was standing on a step-stool, leaning over the sink to the mirror on the medicine cabinet, and smearing on purplish lipstick.

Strewn around them — on the floor, on the back of the toilet, and all around the sink — were cotton balls, Q-tips, hair curlers, and dribs and drabs of leftover makeup, such as the ends of lipsticks, almost empty pots of blusher, and drying tubes of mascara. And seated carefully in a line on the floor were the girls' dolls and teddy bears.

Myriah glanced up and saw her mother and Dawn in the mirror. "Hi!" she called excitedly.

"Hi, Dawn Schafer!" added Gabbie, who calls almost everyone by both first and last name.

"We're having a beauty parlor!" exclaimed Myriah. She put down her lipstick and jumped off the stool. "These are our customers," she said, pointing to the dolls and bears.

"Our customers," echoed Gabbie.

"And now we're fixing ourselves up," said Myriah. "I'm doing my makeup first."

"Girls, I'm going to leave now," Mrs. Perkins interrupted. She turned to Dawn. "I've got another checkup." (Mrs. Perkins is expecting a baby.) "The obstetrician's number is on the refrigerator. I have some errands to run afterward, so I probably won't be home until five o'clock. You know where everything is, right?"

Dawn nodded.

"Any questions?" asked Mrs. Perkins.

"Well," said Dawn, looking around the messy bathroom, "is it *really* okay for the girls to play with all this stuff?"

"Oh, yes. Don't worry about it. I give them the ends of all my makeup. Don't worry about cleaning up, either. We'll do that tonight or tomorrow. They've got a good game going."

Dawn grinned. Mrs. Perkins is great. What a nice mommy. We know this one mommy — Jenny Prezzioso's — who gets hysterical at the very thought of a mess or a little dirt.

After Mrs. Perkins left, Myriah introduced Dawn to some of the "customers" in the beauty parlor. First she held up a bear whose plastic snout was covered with lipstick and who was wearing a shower cap.

"This is Mrs. Xerox," she said. "She's having her hair permed."

"I put her lipstick on," spoke up Gabbie. She had finished her own makeup job and looked at Dawn solemnly from garish eyes. Lipstick, red and pink, stretched from ear to ear. She held up the hand mirror again. "Don't I look pretty? I'm a lovely lady."

"And this," Myriah went on, holding up a baby doll, "is Mrs. Refrigerator. She just needed an eye job. . . . Oh! I better do *my* eyes!"

53

Myriah jumped up on the stool again and began collecting tubes of mascara and eyeliner.

The phone rang.

"Can I get it?" cried Gabbie. She leaped off the toilet, spilling a lapful of hair curlers.

"Better let me," said Dawn. "I'll be right back. You guys keep . . . keep up the good work." She dashed into Mr. and Mrs. Perkins' bedroom and picked up the phone, which was ringing for the third time.

"Hello, Perkins residence," she said.

"Dawn?" asked a disgruntled voice.

"Yes. Jeff? Is that you?"

"Yeah."

"What's up? Are you at home?"

"Not exactly. I'm kind of at school. Using the teachers' phone. And I'm kind of in trouble."

"What do you mean, 'kind of in trouble'?"

"Oh, all right. I *am* in trouble. And Ms. Besser wanted me to call Mom. She won't let me go home until she talks to her. Only I called Mom's office and they said she went to a meeting somewhere in Stamford. So then I remembered you said you were sitting at the Perkinses' and I looked up their number. What should I do now, Dawn?"

"Okay," Dawn said, trying not to get upset,

"let's start at the beginning. Why are you in trouble with Ms. Besser?"

"I threw an eraser across the room. You know, a big blackboard eraser."

"Gosh, that doesn't sound *so* bad. I mean, you shouldn't have done it, but — are you sure that's all you did?"

"It was sort of the third time I threw it across the room. And it knocked over Simon Beal's tile mosaic. And the mosaic broke. And one of the tiles cut Lynn Perone's leg. . . ." Jeff's voice was fading into nothingness.

"Oh, *Jeff*," was all Dawn could say. She paused, thinking. "You're *sure* you can't get in touch with Mom?"

"They said she isn't coming back to the office today. She's going to be in Stamford until five o'clock."

"Well," said Dawn slowly, "I guess I could come to school myself. Maybe I can talk to Ms. Besser or something. I can't let you sit there all afternoon."

"Oh, that'd be great."

"All right. But Jeff, I want you to know I'm not happy about this. I'm baby-sitting. I'll have to bring Myriah and Gabbie with me."

"Okay," replied Jeff, but he didn't say he was sorry.

Dawn returned to the bathroom. "You guys," she said, "I'm really sorry, but we have to close up your beauty parlor for awhile. We've got to go over to your school, Myriah."

"We *do?*" Myriah looked awed. At her age, going to school after hours is kind of like sneaking into an amusement park when it's been closed for the night.

Dawn tried to explain why they had to go, while figuring out the fastest way to get the girls there.

"But let's not *close* the beauty parlor," said Myriah. "Let's take it with us."

"Whatever," replied Dawn, who just wanted to get going fast.

"Goody!" cried Myriah and Gabbie, scooping up makeup and curlers and supplies.

Dawn hustled the girls and their junk downstairs. She didn't have time to wash their faces. She just loaded them and their things into Myriah's red wagon and ran them over to the elementary school in what must have been a wagon-pulling record.

When she reached the front door, she wasn't sure what to do with the wagon, so she pulled the girls right inside and down the hall to Jeff's fifth-grade classroom. She found him sitting sullenly at his desk, while Ms. Besser worked quietly at hers.

"Um, excuse me," said Dawn.

Ms. Besser and Jeff both looked up in surprise at the sight of Myriah and Gabbie in the wagon with their lipstick-smeared faces.

"I'm Dawn Schafer, Jeff's sister." Dawn explained why she had come instead of her mother.

"And *I*," spoke up Myriah, "am Miss Esmerelda. I run a beauty salon. This is my assistant," she added, climbing out of the wagon and pointing to Gabbie.

"I am Miss Gabbie," said Gabbie.

"Would you like a makeover?" Myriah asked Ms. Besser.

"Oh . . . not today, Miss, um — "

"Esmerelda," supplied Myriah. She turned to Jeff. "Would *you* like a makeover? From our traveling beauty parlor?"

"No way," replied Jeff, turning red.

"*I* would like a makeover," Gabbie told her sister.

"Oh, good," said Myriah, and got to work.

Ms. Besser led Dawn into the hall. "I'm very concerned about your brother," she said. "He's gone beyond just being a nuisance or a disturbance in class. If Lynn's cut had been any worse, she would have needed stitches. I wanted to talk to your mother in person. I think we have a serious problem."

"I'm really sorry we can't reach her," said Dawn.

"So am I," Ms. Besser replied.

"I can have her call you tomorrow. Or even at home tonight. Maybe she could set up a conference with you or something."

Ms. Besser nodded. "At the very least. All right. Please do have her call me tonight. I'll give you my home number." She paused. Then she added, "Thank you for taking the trouble to come over here. I can see that it wasn't very convenient for you. You seem quite responsible."

Dawn wasn't sure how to respond to that, so finally she just said "Thank you." A few minutes later she left the school with her brother and the Perkins girls. Jeff immediately headed angrily for home. He had barely spoken to his sister. By the time Dawn and the traveling beauty parlor reached the Perkins house it was 5:15.

Mrs. Perkins met them at the front door. "Where *were* you?" she asked anxiously.

"I'm really sorry," said Dawn. "I should have left a note." She told Mrs. Perkins what had happened, and apologized six or seven times. Luckily, Mrs. Perkins was forgiving and understanding.

* * *

Later, as Dawn pedaled her bike home, she wondered how often she'd have to bail Jeff out of trouble. She flew over a little hump in the road just then, and as she did, pictured herself in a roller coaster, just beginning to pick up speed. Mom, she thought, I have a feeling you and I are in for a bumpy ride.

CHAPTER 7

"I am an artist and my craft is calling," said Ashley earnestly.

"Calling what?" I replied.

"Calling *me*. Like the call of the wild."

It was lunchtime, and Ashley and I were sitting by ourselves again. We had this conversation going, only (and this was so stupid) I didn't know what we were talking about. It's pretty pathetic to be one of the persons in a two-person conversation and not following the drift of things at all.

I glanced across the cafeteria at the Babysitters Club's table and sneaked a peak at Kristy, Stacey, Mary Anne, and Dawn. The usual lunchtime things seemed to be going on. Dawn was eating what looked like homemade fruit salad. Kristy was holding up a noodle from the hot lunch and saying something about it which was making Mary Anne turn green. Stacey was rolling her eyes.

60

I smiled to myself. Kristy always gets gross at lunch and we always give her a hard time about it, but right now I was missing her disgusting comments.

I kind of hoped that one of my friends would look over at me and smile or wave, but none of them did.

I was sitting with Ashley because it was getting to the point where, if I didn't choose a subject for my sculpture and start working right away, I'd have to withdraw from the show. Here's what had led up to Ashley's saying, "I am an artist and my craft is calling":

"Ashley, we really better get to work on our sculptures." (That was me, of course, since, what with baby-sitting and pottery and everything else I do, I'm more pressed for time than Ashley is.)

"Well, I've reached a decision," said Ashley.

"What?" I asked excitedly.

"I'm going to sculpt an inanimate object. I think maybe you should, too."

"You're going to sculpt a what?" (Why is it that when I'm with Ashley, the word that gets the most use is "what"? But Ashley never seems to mind explaining things to me.)

"An inanimate object," Ashley repeated. "Something not alive."

"You want us to sculpt dead things?" I asked

in horror. I was imagining ghouls and corpses and mummies.

"Oh, no. I just mean I want to sculpt objects that aren't living. Look at us. We're surrounded by inanimate objects — books, pencils, tables, chairs, trays. They're all inanimate."

"But," I said skeptically, "I've hardly ever seen sculptures of, um, un-alive things. Aren't most sculptures of people or animals? I mean, except for abstract sculptures. That's what Ms. Baehr says sculpting is all about — capturing the spirit of something alive in something that doesn't move, like clay or stone. . . . I don't know, Ashley. Are you sure we want to go out on a limb like that? Why don't we stick to the more usual stuff?"

And that was when Ashley had said her craft was calling and I'd gotten some good mileage out of the word "what."

"Come downtown with me after school today," she said finally. "We'll go right into the field. I'm sure we'll be inspired."

"What field?" I replied.

"I mean the real world."

"Oh. Well, all right." The "real world" sounded very exciting. Going into the field was probably something only true artists did. A smile spread across my face. We were going to be pioneers, sculpting pioneers. Ashley and

I would try techniques other sculptors had never thought about. I looked across the table at Ashley's serious, eager face. "Great idea," I added. "It'll be exciting. Plus, then we can get to work right away. . . . Oh, but I have another club meeting this afternoon, so I have to be home by five-thirty."

"Sure. No problem," replied Ashley tightly.

Just as going to the watercolor exhibit with Ashley had been an eye-opening experience, so was simply walking around downtown Stoneybrook with her. Maybe because she was new to town, or maybe because she was such a talented artist, Ashley noticed all sorts of things that had never seemed particularly noticeable to me before. And she saw things *in* them that I never saw. Well, never saw first. After Ashley pointed them out to me, I saw them.

As soon as we reached Stoneybrook's main street, Ashley grabbed my arm.

"What, what?" I cried, getting double use of the word.

"Look at that!" said Ashley, pointing.

"What?"

"*That.*"

"That fire hydrant?"

"Yes. Look at the way it's shaped. It's . . .

almost noble. It's little and squat, but it's sitting up straight and square, like a jockey on a prizewinning steed."

"Wow," I said, letting out a breath I hadn't realized I was holding.

"That just might be my subject," said Ashley thoughtfully, nodding her head.

"For your *sculp*ture?" I repeated incredulously. "But why would you sculpt it? What's so special about an old fire hydrant?"

"That it's little but noble. I'd try to bring out those qualities when I sculpt it. I think that the secret of sculpting inanimate objects is making them look animated."

The word "what" was on the tip of my tongue, but I bit it back. When I thought about it, I understood what Ashley meant. I just couldn't see any way to *do* it.

"Come on, let's see what else there is."

Now, over the years I have scoured Stoneybrook in search of a new pair of shoes, in search of a certain kind of blue-jean jacket, in search of school supplies, and once in search of Mary Anne's reading glasses. But this was the first time I'd scoured the town exclaiming over hubcaps and litter baskets and street lamps. I did sort of get into the spirit of things, though.

"Oh!" cried Ashley. "Look at that traffic light!" Ashley sounded more excited that afternoon than I'd ever heard her. It was amazing what art did to her.

"Yeah," I replied. And (I swear I don't know where this came from) I added, "Think of the power it holds. It *controls* the traffic. It can make people late. It can prevent accidents. It's a little box doing an awfully big job."

"Yeah!" said Ashley admiringly. She paused, then added thoughtfully, "Maybe that's your subject."

"Maybe," I replied uncertainly.

We walked on.

"Look at the gum wrapper," said Ashley.

"Look at that squashed soda can," I said.

By the time we sat down in Renwick's for a snack, all I could say was, "Look at that straw!" and "Look at that dish rag!" Stuff like that. Until I checked my watch. Then I cried, "Look at the time!"

"What time is it?" asked Ashley.

"Five-ten. I'm going to be late for another meeting. I'm sorry, but I've got to leave."

"But Claudia, we haven't made any definite decisions. We have to go back and look at the fire hydrant and the stoplight again."

"I *have* to go to the meeting. The club is

important to me. We started that club. We made it work. It's a business. And besides, the other club members are my friends."

Ashley blinked. "But I'm your friend, too . . . am I not?" she said, sounding like my genius sister, Janine. (I have this older sister who's a genius. Not just smart, like Ashley, but a true and honest genius. How is it that I always end up hanging around people who know enough to say things like "am I not" instead of "aren't I"?)

"Yes," I replied slowly. "You're my friend."

Ashley gave me a tiny smile. I began to feel bad. Maybe I was really important to her. I wasn't sure. I was *pretty* sure I was her only friend, though. I had four good friends, but so far, Ashley only had me. Besides, this was art. What Ashley and I were doing was important — and it was something I could do only with Ashley, not with any of my other friends.

"You know," I said, "that meeting isn't urgent or anything. We really should go back and look at the fire hydrant and stoplight again. Why don't you wait for our food while I call Dawn and tell her I won't be able to make the meeting. I'll be right back."

I stood in the phone booth by the front door of Renwick's and dialed Dawn's number, hoping fervently that she was at home and not out baby-sitting. I breathed a sigh of relief when she answered the phone herself.

"Hi," I said. "It's me, Claudia."

"Oh, hi," replied Dawn lightly, but there was a cautious edge to her voice.

"Listen," I told her, "I'm not going to be able to make the meeting today. Ashley and I *have* to choose subjects for our sculptures — you know, for the show. So can you be the vice-president for me today?"

"Sure."

"And tell the others that I won't be coming."

"Sure."

An embarrassing pause followed.

Finally Dawn said, "Do you want us to sign you up for any jobs? I mean, are your art classes and things on the appointment pages so we know when you're busy?"

"I think so," I said. "Well, I better go before my money runs out. I'm downtown in a pay phone."

"Okay," said Dawn shortly. " 'Bye."

She hung up before I could answer her.

With a sigh, I returned to Ashley, who greeted me with a smile.

That evening I read, for the fifth time, the note Mary Anne, as club secretary, had left for me after the meeting which had been held in my room that afternoon: Claudia — you're sitting for Nina and Eleanor Marshall next Friday from 3:30–6:00. — M.A.S.

That was it. The entire note. No "Hi, Claud!" or "See you soon," or anything. I guess my friends were mad at me. By the time I went to bed, I was sure of it. That was because, hidden under my pillow, I found a note from Kristy which said: Everyone at school thinks Ashley is weird. I just thought you should know. — Kristy.

The worst thing about the day was that I hadn't even chosen a subject for my sculpture. Ashley had chosen the fire hydrant, but I just couldn't bring myself to sculpt a stoplight. Not even in order to become a sculpture pioneer. I had missed a meeting, wasted an afternoon, and was no closer to entering the art show than before.

CHAPTER 8

Some people around here are TRAITORS. And you know who you are. Ordinarily, this notebook is used to record our baby-sitting jobs, but it's also for club problems, and we have a little problem right now. The little problem is a certain person who keeps missing meetings. It's a good thing we have an alternate officer because Dawn sure has had to take over the duties of our vice-president a lot lately.

But I don't mind being vice-president, you guys.

Okay, so Dawn doesn't mind, but we do mind having a V.P. who'd rather be an artist.

Yeah, our V.P. used to be very nice, but now she never shows up at meetings and she hangs around with a person who wears BELL-BOTTOM BLUE JEANS to school.

Kristy's notebook entry went on for so long that I got a pretty complete idea of what happened at the second club meeting that I couldn't attend. Plus, later — when we were friends again — Stacey filled me in on every little thing I'd missed.

But I'm getting ahead of myself. What made me miss another meeting was that Ashley convinced me to take a second inspirational walk in "the field" with her, looking for something to sculpt, since I couldn't bring myself to sculpt the traffic light. We ran late again, I had to call Dawn to ask her to take over my duties, and another meeting was held in my room without me.

The meeting started out with Dawn running into my room, arriving just after Kristy had, and announcing, "Well, I'm the vice-president again today."

"You are?" Kristy said. "How come?"

"Claudia just called. She and Ashley are doing something."

"*What?*" demanded Kristy.

"I don't know. It has to do with that sculpture show."

Kristy, mumbling and grumbling, began pawing around my bed, lifting up my pillow

70

and comforter, and finally sliding off the bed headfirst and peering underneath it.

"What are you doing?" asked Dawn.

"Looking for Claudia's Bazooka bubblegum. I know she's got some stashed somewhere."

Mary Anne entered my room then, followed by Stacey. "What are you doing?" she asked Kristy. (Everyone seemed to want to know.)

"Looking for Claudia's bubblegum."

"It's in her hollow book," said Stacey, pointing to the bookshelf. "Where's Claudia?"

"Three guesses," replied Kristy, biting off the words angrily. She pulled the hollow book from my shelf. (It's my best, most clever hiding place ever.) Then she reached in, pulled out two pieces of gum (one for her, one for Mary Anne — Dawn and Stacey won't touch the stuff), and began chewing.

"I only need one guess," said Stacey, "and it isn't a guess. It's a 'know.' She's with Ashley again."

"Right."

"Ha." Stacey flumped onto my bed. "Ashley was wearing *bell-bottoms* today. Everyone was talking about her."

"She is so weird," said Mary Anne. "She doesn't talk to anyone but Claudia. I think she's stuck-up."

Ring, ring.

My friends were slower than usual in answering the phone. Stacey picked it up after three rings and arranged a job sitting for Jamie and Lucy Newton. Then Dawn's mother called needing a sitter for Jeff one evening.

"How are things going with Jeff?" Mary Anne asked Dawn after she'd finished talking with Mrs. Schafer.

Dawn shrugged. "Okay, I guess. Mom had a conference with his teacher and told her what's going on with Jeff at home. Then Ms. Besser told her what Jeff was doing in school. Like, *not* working, *not* bothering to raise his hand. All these *nots*. They've decided that they're just going to try being very firm with him and not letting him get away with a thing. And really praise him for the good stuff he does. That doesn't sound like much to me. I thought they were going to talk about bigger things, like whether Jeff should move back to California to be with Dad. But I guess you start with something small and hope it will do the trick."

"Sure," said Mary Anne. "It's like giving a sick person a pill instead of going ahead and doing a whole huge operation."

The girls had to laugh at Mary Anne's comparison. The idea of Jeff on an operating table

72

having his bad humor removed was pretty funny.

"But," Dawn went on thoughtfully a few moments later, "Mom and Dad have been talking a lot lately."

"About Jeff?" asked Stacey.

"Probably. The only reason I know is because I was in Mom's desk the other day looking for Scotch tape, and the phone bill was right on top of a pile of stuff. I didn't even have to snoop to see all the calls that have been made to Dad's number. It was a whole long list of them. All from the last few weeks, and most of them late at night. I guess they're talking at night because they don't want Jeff and me to know what they're discussing. Which means the subject must be Jeff. What else could be so important to both of them? They're sure not going to get remarried or anything."

"What do you think they're saying?" asked Mary Anne in a small voice.

Dawn shook her head. "I . . . I don't know. . . ."

The phone rang and Dawn leapt for it, as if she were glad for the chance to avoid Mary Anne's question. "Hello, Baby-sitters Club," she said. "Yes? . . . Yes. . . . Okay. . . . Okay. . . . Until eleven? Well, I'll check and get back to you. . . . Right. . . . 'Bye."

Mary Anne, always organized and ready, was waiting with the record book in her lap by the time Dawn hung up the phone. It was open to the appointment pages. "A night job?" she asked, her eyes shining. We all love baby-sitting late at night, even though sometimes we get scared.

"Yup," replied Dawn. "At the Papadak-ises'."

"When?" asked Mary Anne.

Dawn told her.

"Well, let's see. Kristy, you're free, and so's Claudia," said Mary Anne.

"Oh, give the job to Kristy," said Dawn and Stacey together. The two of them were so busy being smug about the thought of not giving the job to *me*, that they didn't even bother to hook pinkies and say "jinx."

The thing is, the Papadakises live over in Kristy's neighborhood, and we usually let Kristy take jobs that are near to her because it's so much more convenient for both her and our clients if nobody has to drive anywhere. But at that meeting, it was plain that my friends didn't want me to get the job. They were punishing me for not being at the meeting.

Mary Anne wrote Kristy's job on the ap-pointment calendar, while Dawn called Mrs. Papadakis back and told her that Kristy would be sitting. When she hung up, Mary Anne said, sounding guilty, "Do you think we should have offered that job to Claudia, too? We could have called Mrs. Papadakis tomorrow."

"No way," said Stacey. "Why make a good client wait? Besides, Kristy usually sits for the people in her neighborhood. We do that on purpose. Right, Kristy?"

"Right," she agreed.

For a moment, nobody spoke.

Then Stacey said, "Claudia probably wouldn't even have *time* to sit. She's so busy with Ashley."

"She hasn't eaten lunch with us in days," added Dawn.

"I don't think she likes me anymore," said Stacey softly.

Mary Anne was looking sympathetically at Stacey. As Stacey's eyes filled with tears, so did Mary Anne's.

"*Darn* it," cried Stacey, mashing her fist into my pillow and smushing a package of cookies that was hidden underneath. "I *hate* crying."

"It's okay," whimpered Mary Anne, edging closer to Stacey. "We don't mind if you cry. We know Claudia's your best friend. You must feel . . . terrible. . . ." Mary Anne's tears spilled down her cheeks before Stacey's did.

"Oh, this is just *fine*," exclaimed Kristy.

"Claudia's not even here, and look what she's turned this meeting into. A cry-fest. Where are Claudia's Twinkies? I know they're here somewhere. I need a Twinkie. I'm having a Twinkie attack." Kristy was practically destroying my room in her search for junk food. It was so silly. Anyone with half a brain would know I keep the Twinkies in my sock drawer.

"Mary Anne, get a grip on yourself," said Stacey, who'd already stopped crying. "Think of pleasant things. Think of Tigger." (Tigger is Mary Anne's kitten.)

"Think of Shannon," said Kristy. (Shannon is the Thomas kids' new puppy.)

"Think of Logan," said Dawn. (Logan is Mary Anne's boyfriend. Believe it or not, she's the only club member who has a boyfriend.)

"I'm trying," said Mary Anne, sniffling.

"Oh, brother," said Kristy. "Listen to us. 'Think lovely thoughts.' Do you know who we sound like? We sound like Peter Pan, that's who. Peter *Pan*. We are baby-sitters, not magical, flying boys. Now, you guys."

"Yes?" said Dawn, Stacey, and Mary Anne.

"Dry your eyes, sit up straight, wait for the phone to ring, quit thinking like Peter Pan, and — *behave like baby-sitters*."

CHAPTER 9

I slammed my locker closed, heard a rustling sound inside, and immediately wrenched my locker open again. I knew what had happened. My poster of Max Morrison, the most gorgeous star in the history of television, had fallen off the inside of the door. This happens about once a day. At Stoneybrook Middle School you're not allowed to put things up in the lockers with tape, so us kids get around this by using bits of chewed-up gum. The only problem is, the gum loses its stickiness after awhile.

I smacked the poster back onto the gum bits, reminding myself to chew up some new gum soon, and closed my locker again. Then I turned around and nearly ran into Ashley. She was wearing a long, all-the-way-to-her-ankles dress with three rows of ruffles at the bottom. A strip of black cloth was tied around her head. I couldn't see her earrings, but she looked

. . . well, all right, I'll admit it. She looked a little bizarre.

"I'm glad I found you," said Ashley. "I had a great idea this morning — for your sculpture — and I wanted to tell you about it right away."

"Thank goodness," I said, "because I'm not too sure about an, um, inanimate object."

"I know — " Ashley began.

"Hi, Claudia."

"Hi, Claudia."

"Hi, Claudia."

"Hi, Claudia."

I turned around. There were the other members of the Baby-sitters Club. I was really glad they'd come to talk. They hardly ever do that when Ashley's around.

"Hi, you guys!" I replied. I waited for my friends to say hi to Ashley or for Ashley to say hi to my friends, but none of them spoke.

"Well . . ." I said nervously.

"We missed you at the meeting yesterday," said Kristy pointedly.

"I'm sorry. I had to think about — "

"We know, we know. Your sculpture," said Dawn.

Stacey eyed Ashley critically. "Nice dress," she commented.

Ashley flushed with embarrassment, but she didn't reply. We all knew Stacey was being sarcastic.

"Do you suppose you'll be able to clear time in your busy schedule to get to the next meeting?" Dawn asked me.

I looked at her in surprise. What kind of question was that from our even-tempered alternate officer?

"I plan to," was all I replied.

"I hope *you* approve of that," said Kristy to Ashley.

Ashley still looked awfully uncomfortable. "Claudia," she began uncertainly, and then seemed to gain some confidence. "Claudia is an artist — "

"Don't remind us," interrupted Kristy.

"She's an artist," Ashley went on, "and she needs to spend time on her work."

"What are you? Her tutor or something?" asked Stacey.

"I'm her mentor," replied Ashley, as serious as always.

Well, that put a stop to things for a moment or two because only Ashley knew what a mentor was. (I looked it up in the dictionary later. It means a wise and trusted teacher. I guess that's better than a plain old tutor.)

"If Claudia is going to develop her talents

to the fullest — and I do think she can go a long way in the world of art — "

(I beamed again. I couldn't help it. You just don't shrug off compliments like that one.)

" — she has to devote as much time as possible to her art," Ashley finished.

"But she does," insisted Mary Anne. "Plenty of time." And I thought, my friends really don't understand, do they?

Ashley shook her head. "Spending time on anything else, especially baby-sitting, is just a waste."

"Hey," said Kristy, turning angrily to me, "does this mean you're quitting the club? It would be nice if you'd let us know. We'd like to hold the meetings somewhere other than in your room, if you are. And of course we'll have to give our clients our new phone number, make up new fliers, all sorts of things."

"I'm not quitting the club!" I exclaimed.

"Could have fooled us," said Stacey.

"Yeah," spoke up Mary Anne, sounding unusually fierce.

"We could use a little warning if you are," said Kristy.

"I AM NOT QUITTING!" I cried.

"Good," said Kristy and Stacey.

"Good," I said.

"Good-*bye*," added Dawn and Mary Anne.

"Good-*bye*," I replied.

My four friends turned and walked off down the hall. I was left standing with Ashley. "Oh, who needs them anyway?" I said grumpily.

"Right," agreed Ashley. "Who needs friends when you have art?"

I tried to smile at Ashley, but it was difficult.

"Ew, ew! Get away from me! Get *away!*" shrieked Fiona McRae.

"Ooo-eeee-oooo. You'll never escape the Mud Monster from the deep." John Steiner, his hands dripping with watered-down clay, chased Fiona around the room.

This is the sort of thing that usually goes on at our art class if Ms. Baehr arrives a few minutes late. John and Fiona weren't the only kids acting up. Seth Turbin was making fake eyeballs out of his clay, and Mari Drabek was trying to fashion a pair of glasses for the eyeballs.

I kept looking around and giggling — especially at the eyeballs and glasses — but Ashley sat stiffly in front of her fire hydrant sculpture. She worked busily, not even aware of the other kids. I wished I could be as focused as Ashley was.

"Good afternoon, class!" called Ms. Baehr's voice.

We snapped to attention. John ran to the sink — as if that's where he'd been headed all along — to clean up his hands. Seth and Mari smashed their eyeballs and glasses flat. And everyone else flew into their seats. (Except for Ashley, who was already in her seat.)

"While you're working today," Ms. Baehr said, ignoring all the confusion, "I want to find out how each of you is doing with your piece for the show. I'll walk around and talk to you privately. Feel free to interrupt me if you need help with anything."

Since Ashley and I were at the worktable in the front of the room, Ms. Baehr approached us first. "Ashley?" she said. "You've definitely decided to go ahead with the fire hydrant?"

"Yes," replied Ashley. "And this is it. I mean, the beginning of it." She indicated the lumpy clay that was slowly gaining form in front of her.

Ms. Baehr looked at it for several seconds. Her face was expressionless. At last she said, "You do realize that this is an odd choice for a sculpture, don't you?"

Ashley frowned. "Well," she said slowly, "I think it's just different. I want to do something different."

"Wouldn't you like to finish up the eagle you started? It was lovely. It would be perfect for the show."

"No." said Ashley. "It's too . . . commonplace. I really want to make a statement with my work."

Ashley bit her lip and I knew she was afraid that Ms. Baehr would tell her she couldn't work on the fire hydrant. But I kept wondering what kind of statement a fire hydrant would make. I could tell Ms. Baehr was wondering the same thing. She usually keeps an open mind, though, so all she said was, "Very well."

Then she turned to me.

I was working on my hand sculpture again, and Ms. Baehr said, "Beautiful, Claudia. That's coming along fine."

"What, this?" I replied. "This is just a practice piece. It's not for the show. I don't know what I'm going to enter."

"You'd better choose soon, Claud, and then get cracking," said Ms. Baehr kindly. "But I like the hand. Why not enter it?"

"I — I want to make a statement, too," I said with a sidelong glance at Ashley.

Ashley smiled. I knew she was pleased that I was listening to her, my mentor.

But Ms. Baehr sighed. "Okay, Claud." She

straightened up and walked over to Fiona McRae's table.

"Hey, I'm proud of you!" Ashley said to me, speaking softly so Ms. Baehr wouldn't hear.

"Really?" I replied, glowing.

"Yes. And — well, I never got to tell you the idea I had this morning. We got interrupted by your, um, friends. My idea is that if you don't want to sculpt an inanimate object, you could make a statement by sculpting a concept."

"What?" (There was that word again. Thank goodness someone had invented it.)

"You know, sculpt 'love' or 'peace' or 'brotherhood.' "

"I . . ." I had absolutely no idea how to do that and no idea what to say to Ashley.

"Oh, don't worry. I don't mind if you use my idea. Really."

"Well, I . . . um, I don't know what to say. Um . . . I'm speechless."

Ashley laughed. "I think you should try it. Anyone who can see power in a stoplight ought to be able to come up with a great visual representation of a concept."

I cleared my throat. "Oh, right. How — how would *you* sculpt 'love'?"

"With gentle curves and tender feelings."

84

Well, that was no help.

"Hmm," I said. "I'll think about it." I turned back to my hand. What I *really* needed to think about was how to tell Ashley that I wasn't going to sculpt a nonliving thing or an idea. I just couldn't do either one. The problem was how to tell her without looking too stupid.

"Hey, Claud?"

"Yeah?"

"Do you want to come over to my house sometime? I could show you some of the sculptures I'm working on at home. And also the studio my parents are having fixed up for me. It's on the top floor of our house, where the best light is. I'll be able to paint and draw and sculpt there. A whole room for my work."

"Gosh, that's great!" I exclaimed. "Sure I'll come. I'd love to see everything."

My doubts were replaced with excitement. Ashley, a great artist, liked me and valued me and trusted me. What else could you want in a friend?

CHAPTER 10

All right, so how many meetings do you plan to miss, Ms. Artist? How many shopping dates do you plan to skip out on? And what does "friend" mean to you, anyway? To me, it means somebody who keeps up her half of certain bargains, who keeps in touch with you -- calls you from time to time and eats lunch with you. And who doesn't LIE or BREAK DATES. It means somebody who doesn't forget her old friends just because someone new comes along, whether that someone is a girl, or a boy as gorgeous as Max Morrison.

I don't feel that you're my friend anymore. Or that you want me for yours.

Boy, does Stacey know how to bring tears to a person's eyes. Maybe if I'd read her entry sooner, things among us club members wouldn't have gotten just as bad as they did. But not only had I been missing meetings, I hadn't kept up with our club notebook.

Furthermore, I had done something terrible to Stacey. I hadn't meant to, exactly. But it had happened. At the end of school one day, Stacey asked me to go to the mall with her. I told her I couldn't because I had to catch up on some English assignments. That was true. I was really (*really*) planning to go to the library. But on the way there I ran into Ashley, who invited me to her house. Since I needed to discuss my sculpture subject with her, I went. I forgot all about Stacey. I forgot so completely, in fact, that when I called Dawn to tell her I'd have to miss that afternoon's meeting, I also told her why.

That was my big mistake. (Well, one of them.)

Let me tell you, I didn't feel good about missing club meetings and spending so little time with my friends. But I felt great having a mentor who liked my work so much and thought I was smart and kept telling me how much artistic potential I had. When you're a C-student who has to go to the Resource Room, "potential" is a word you don't hear a lot, unless someone, usually a teacher or guidance counselor or one of your parents, says, "It's really a shame. I don't see why her grades aren't better. She does have potential. . . ."

But I'm getting way off the subject. I wanted to tell you about the next meeting of the Baby-sitters Club — the next one I missed, that is. It started, as usual, with my friends coming over to my house and being greeted by Mimi. Mimi told them to go straight to my room, even though I wasn't there. She understands how important the club is, and she really likes my friends. It might have seemed funny to Kristy, Stacey, Dawn, and Mary Anne to be in my room without me, but it was okay with Mimi.

I had called Dawn around five o'clock that day. She had seemed quite cool, but, well, you'd think she'd enjoy the chance to be a real officer instead of just sort of an officer-in-waiting . . . wouldn't you?

She didn't seem too thrilled, though, and told me later that as she biked over to my house for the meeting, a mean little rhyme kept running through her head:

Traitor, traitor.
Claudia — we hate 'er!
Traitor, traitor.
So long, see you later!
Good-bye, Claudia.

Dawn and Kristy reached my house first, and as soon as Mimi ushered them inside, they ran to my room. Stacey arrived next. She stood in the doorway of my room, looked at Dawn sprawled on my bed and Kristy reading the notebook, and said, "Okay, where is she?"

"You mean Claudia?" replied Dawn.

"Who else?"

"She's at Ashley's."

"Ashley's?!" Stacey's face turned the color of a pomegranate. "That big liar! Are you sure? She told me she couldn't go to the mall with me this afternoon because she had to study at the library."

"You're kidding," said Kristy.

"I'm dead serious," replied Stacey, who became so mad then that she couldn't even speak. That was when she took our notebook (grabbed it right out of Kristy's hands) and started writing all that stuff about friendship.

Mary Anne showed up at five-thirty on the dot. "Hi, you gu — " she started to say. Then she narrowed her eyes. "Is *she* missing again?" she asked.

"Ha," said Kristy. "Very good, Sherlock Holmes."

"Hey, don't snap at me," retorted Mary Anne, sticking up for herself for once. "*I* didn't skip another meeting. *I'm* here on time."

"Sorry," said Kristy contritely.

"You know what I feel like doing?" said Stacey, setting the diary aside. "I feel like raiding Claudia's junk food. It would serve her right if she came back and found we'd eaten everything."

"But you can't eat that stuff!" Dawn exclaimed.

"I can eat some of it," Stacey replied. "I can eat her pretzels and her crackers — not too many, of course. And I know where they're hidden. Pretzels in that old pyjama bag, crackers in the Monopoly box."

"I wouldn't mind eating up some of her stuff," said Kristy with a slow grin. "Let's see, she's got marshmallows in that shoe box and licorice sticks under her mattress."

"*I'll* even help you eat that junk," said Dawn, making, for her, a supreme sacrifice.

"Well, I'll help, too," said Mary Anne. "And, hey! After we're done? We should take whatever's left and put it back in the wrong places!"

My friends began giggling but had to calm down when the phone rang three times with job calls. When the sitters were all lined up, Stacey began raiding my junk food. She tossed the licorice sticks to Mary Anne, the marshmallows to Kristy, the pretzels to Dawn, and took the crackers for herself. My friends ate for awhile, then stopped to switch food. Dawn actually wolfed down three marshmallows, but then made a big deal out of having to rinse her mouth out so she wouldn't get cavities.

When they couldn't eat anymore, Stacey said, "Okay, now take what's left and put it away — where it doesn't belong."

Mary Anne stuffed the bag with the few remaining marshmallows in one of my sneakers.

Kristy stuck the licorice sticks into the back of a bureau drawer.

Dawn hid the crackers in a purse I don't use anymore.

And Stacey saw my old black fedora on the shelf in my closet and put the pretzels underneath it.

Then my friends began laughing hysterically.

(That night, it took me almost an hour to find everything. Plus, a bag of Doritos is still missing, but no one will tell me if they had anything to do with that.)

The club members had to calm down, though, when Mrs. Perkins called needing a sitter for Myriah and Gabbie, and Mrs. Delaney called needing a sitter for Amanda and Max.

But as soon as that business was taken care of, Kristy said, "Let's short-sheet her bed!" They didn't even use my name anymore. They just called me "she" or "her" and knew who they meant.

So Kristy and Mary Anne short-sheeted my bed. Was I ever mad that night when I discovered what they'd done! I was dead tired because I'd stayed up late trying to catch up on my homework and read *The Twenty-One Balloons* (another Newbery book). By the time I was ready to go to bed, I was so sleepy I could barely turn my comforter back. When I did, and I slid between the sheets, my legs only went halfway down. I kicked around. I couldn't imagine what was wrong. Finally I lifted up my comforter and looked. I couldn't believe it! Pinned to the sheet was a note that read: Ha, ha! Sleep tight!

It wasn't the only note I found. That was because while Kristy and Mary Anne had been working on my bed that afternoon, Stacey had said, "Hey, Dawn, let's hide some notes for Claudia to find."

"Notes? What kind of notes?"

"Mean ones."

Stacey ripped a sheet of paper out of the club notebook. Then she stopped to think, tapping a pencil against her mouth. Finally she wrote: Roses are red, violets are blue, traitors are jerks, and so are you.

"Now what?" asked Dawn.

"I think I'll put it under her pillow."

Dawn grinned. Then she tore a piece of paper out of the book and wrote down the rhyme she'd made up earlier. I found that note in my jewelry box.

It was Kristy's idea to hide a blank piece of paper under Lennie, my rag doll.

"What for?" asked Stacey.

"To drive her crazy. She'll wonder if we used invisible ink, or maybe wrote something so mean we had to erase it."

Stacey began giggling. But she had to get herself under control when the phone rang. A new client was calling. Stacey took down the information we needed and got the man squared away with a sitter for his twin girls. Then she said, very seriously, "You guys, why do you think Ashley Wyeth wants Claudia to be her friend so badly?"

"What do you mean?" asked Mary Anne,

after a pause. "She just wants a friend, doesn't she? She's new here. She doesn't know anyone."

"I guess what I mean is, why *only* Claudia? Doesn't it seem that she wants just one friend and that friend is Claudia?"

"Yeah," said Dawn slowly. "I see what you mean, Stace. When I first moved here, I wanted friends — in general. It was great when you and I got to know each other, Mary Anne, but it wasn't like I wanted just one friend and once I had you I was happy. I was really glad when you introduced me to the rest of the club. I had a bunch of friends in California, and when we moved, I hoped I'd have a bunch in Connecticut, too."

"Exactly," said Stacey. "I felt the same way when I moved from New York. I met Claud first and we're still best friends . . . I think. But I was really happy to meet all of you, too. Plus Pete and Howie and Dori and everyone we ate lunch with last year. But Ashley doesn't seem to want any friends except Claud."

"Yeah, she hardly ever speaks to us," added Dawn.

"She doesn't pay much attention to anyone but Claudia. She doesn't talk to other kids, either. If she didn't eat lunch with Claudia," said Stacey, "I'm sure she'd eat alone."

"Ashley's in my gym class," spoke up Mary Anne. "She's always alone. You know, I think all Ashley really cares about is art, and she's found a good artist in Claudia. Maybe Claudia is sort of a project for Ashley." Mary Anne paused, putting her hands in her lap and staring down at them. "Oh, I'm not explaining myself very well."

"You're explaining yourself fine," said Stacey. "What you just said is that Ashley likes Claud because she's an artist, not because she's Claud. And if that's true, I'm beginning to wonder just how good a friend Ashley Wyeth is."

CHAPTER 11

"Whoops," said Jackie Rodowsky.

You know how I'd be absolutely lost without the word "what"? Well, Jackie would be absolutely lost without "whoops," "oops," and "uh-oh."

I hadn't really been doing much baby-sitting lately. Since I kept missing meetings, I wasn't signed up for many jobs. But I'd been signed up for this afternoon with the Rodowsky boys for quite some time, and to tell you the truth, I'd really been looking forward to it. Jackie might be accident-prone, but whenever his mother comes home and finds something broken or a spill on the carpet or a Band-Aid on Jackie's finger, she never minds. Well, of course she's concerned if Jackie hurts himself, but she never gives me, as the baby-sitter, any grief. I guess she's used to such things.

Besides, there's something about Jackie's freckles and his shock of red hair and his great big grin with one tooth missing that always makes me want to grin, too. Even if Jackie's holding out a toy he's broken or is coming to tell me he's just accidentally poured glue over the telephone.

So I had looked forward to sitting for the Rodowskys that day. Nevertheless, I glanced up warily at the sound of Jackie's "whoops" that afternoon. I knew it meant trouble of some sort. I was in the kitchen rinsing off dishes from the boys' afternoon snack. As I shut off the water, I heard the vacuum cleaner being turned off.

"Jackie?" I called. "Archie? Shea?"

"Um, we're in the dining room," said Shea as the vacuum cleaner whined into silence. Shea sounded as if he were admitting to the Great Train Robbery.

I dashed into the dining room. There I found Jackie peering into the hose of the vacuum cleaner as Shea and Archie looked on guiltily. All three boys were barefoot. Their shoes were lined up under the dining room table.

"What is going on?" I asked, trying not to sound too exasperated.

"We tried a speriment," said Jackie. "And guess what? You can vacuum up socks."

"Socks?!" I exclaimed. "Did you vacuum up *all* of your socks?"

"Six of 'em," said Archie. "Three pairs, six socks."

I groaned.

"We didn't mean to, exactly," spoke up Shea. "They were in a pile. We thought maybe the vacuum would just get one, but they all went. Whoosh, whoosh, whoosh, whoosh, whoosh, whoosh," he said, demonstrating with his hands.

"Shea, really. You're the oldest," I said, knowing that didn't mean a thing. (Why should it?)

"It was Jackie's idea," he countered.

"Well, what did you plan to do about your sock if it was vacuumed up?" I asked Jackie.

"See what happened to it," he replied simply.

This wasn't getting us anywhere. "All right," I said, sighing. "The next thing to do is find the socks."

"Goody!" cried Jackie, jumping up and down. "I wonder what they'll look like."

"Maybe the Vacuum Monster attacked them. Maybe they'll be all chewed up," suggested Archie.

I was just dying to ask Archie what he thought the Vacuum Monster was, but I didn't want to start anything. Instead, I lifted the cover of the vacuum, pulled out the dusty bag at the back, and headed into the kitchen with it. The boys trailed behind me.

"What are you going to do?" asked Jackie.

"Cut it open and see what's inside," I replied.

"Awesome," said Shea.

I took a look. Nothing but a cloud of dust.

"Ew, gross," said Jackie, and sneezed.

I threw the bag away and returned to the vacuum cleaner. I noticed that the boys hadn't put an attachment on the end of the hose. Gingerly I reached into the hose as far as possible, which really wasn't very far, and withdrew my hand, a sock between my fingers. The sock was rumpled but otherwise fine.

The Rodowskys looked on in surprise.

"I wonder why the Vacuum Monster didn't want it," said Archie.

"Some experiment," commented Shea.

It took more than fifteen minutes, but after poking, prodding, and digging around with a pair of toast tongs, I managed to remove all the socks from the hose.

"Will you guys promise me something?" I said as they put their socks and shoes back on.

"What?" asked Jackie.

"That you won't use the vacuum again without asking me first."

"Promise," they replied.

"Thank you. Now let's do something fun."

"Let's watch *Sesame Street*," said Archie.

"Wouldn't you rather play a game?" I asked.

"Red Light, Green Light!" cried Jackie. "Please, Claudia?"

"Well . . ." I replied, remembering my vow not to play stupid games in the Rodowskys' front yard anymore.

"Puh-*lease?*" added Archie. "That was fun. Can I be the policeman?"

I hadn't even answered the boys and already they were racing for the front door.

I followed them. Red Light, Green Light it would be. That was my responsibility as their baby-sitter.

Jackie threw the front door open. Standing on the stoop was Ashley, her hand poised to ring the bell.

Despite the fact that the boys had been somewhat awed by her the first time they met her, Jackie began jumping up and down. "Hi!" he cried. "We're going to play Red Light, Green Light again. You want to play?"

He pushed open the screen door and squeezed by Ashley, jumping down the steps (and nar-

100

rowly missing the hedge that lined the front walk).

Archie followed, calling, "But you can't be the policeman. I'm the policeman first. That's my job today!"

Shea was the last one out the door. Just before he leaped down all four stairs in a single bound, he turned and said, "Claudia's the best police officer, though. Right, Claudia?"

Luckily, he wasn't really expecting an answer.

I stepped onto the front porch, closing the doors behind me.

Ashley looked at me, an eyebrow raised.

"Red Light, Green Light again?" she asked.

I tried to laugh. "They love it," I replied.

Ashley frowned. "I just don't understand why you waste all your time on . . ." (she held her hand toward the Rodowskys, who were gearing up for the game) ". . . all this."

I paused. "All *what*?" I finally said, somewhat testily.

"This uselessness."

"They're children," I replied quietly. "They're important to me."

"Oh, you sound so sentimental," Ashley scoffed, looking at the ground.

"Sentimental doesn't sound so bad for an

artist. Artists are very *feeling* people. They have to put their emotions into their work."

Ashley didn't respond and I realized this was the first time I'd ever tried to tell *her* something about art.

"Besides," I went on, as Ashley fidgeted with the ruffles on her peasant blouse, "who was the one who said she'd sculpt 'love' with gentle curves and tender feelings? That's pure mush if I ever heard it."

"Mush?!"

"Sentiment, soft stuff, you know."

Ashley's ice-blue eyes turned icier. "This is the thanks I get for — "

"For what, Ashley? What did you do that you expect thanks for? What did you do that you wouldn't have done just because you're my friend?"

"I taught you about sculpting. I taught you how to look beyond Ms. Baehr and see what else you can do."

"And you think you deserve to be paid back? You think I owe you something? Friendship doesn't work that way. Friends are friends because they like each other, not because they're in debt," I said. I was angry, but I didn't raise my voice. I didn't want to upset the Rodowskys.

"I *do* like you," replied Ashley, and for the

first time since I'd met her, I thought she looked, well, not in control. Her chin quivered and her voice quivered and her eyes filled with tears. "I do want you to be my friend," she added.

"But you want me to devote my life to art. And that's not fair. You shouldn't make up conditions for friendship. Besides, there's more to my life than you and art. I'm not giving anything up."

Ashley regained her cool as quickly as she'd lost it. "You mean, you're not giving anything up *just for me.* Because I'm not important enough to you. That's what you're saying, isn't it? Well, I'll tell you something, Claudia Kishi. You are ungrateful. And foolish. And you don't know a thing about being a friend."

With a swish of her hair, her eyes flashing, Ashley spun around and marched down the steps and across the yard to her house. She left me standing on the Rodowskys' porch, feeling like an empty sack that had once held something nice, like dried flowers, and was now slowly being filled with rocks. And each rock was an unpleasant thought:

Clunk: She's right. I haven't been a good friend. At least, not to Stacey and the other members of the Baby-sitters Club.

Clunk: Everyone must hate me.

Clunk: I wish I could talk to Stacey, but I'd be surprised if she ever speaks to me again.

"Hey, you guys," I called to Jackie, Shea, and Archie. "Come on inside, okay? Red Light, Green Light wasn't a very good idea after all. It looks like it's going to rain."

The boys came inside with only a little grumbling. I settled them in front of the TV in the rec room, and then went to the living room to think. I needed to be alone for a while. What had happened to me over the past couple of weeks? Somehow I'd allowed myself to be swept away by Ashley. Did I have any other friends now? Before Ashley came along, I'd call Stacey when I was upset about something. Now I couldn't do that. And what about the art show? Ms. Baehr expected me to enter. I'd told my parents I was going to enter. And I didn't even have a subject for the sculpture.

"Claudia?"

My thoughts were interrupted by Jackie. He approached me with one sneaker on, the other in his hand, the laces bunched into a huge tangle.

"Can you help me?" he asked, holding out the sneaker. He was smiling his great smile.

"Of course," I answered.

And as I worked at the knot, I suddenly

thought: Jackie. I'll sculpt Jackie. He'd be a great subject. I've been wanting to sculpt something "alive" all along.

I gave Jackie a grin and was rewarded with another of his gap-toothed ones.

CHAPTER 12

What an interesting afternoon this turned out to be. I was sitting for the Rodowskys' and Claudia came over. This was totally unexpected. I'm pretty sure she didn't know I was going to be there. (After all, when was the last time she looked at the appointment calendar in the record book?) Claudia tried to hide her surprise when I answered the door. And I tried to hide my annoyance. We both succeeded. Anyway, it turns out she wants to sculpt Jackie. She had just started making a sketch of him when the doorbell rang again. This time it was Ashley! I think Claudia and Ashley had had a fight. Then they sort of had another one in front of Jackie and me. Things were getting "curiouser and curiouser." Thank goodness Claudia filled me in on everything, or I would have died from wondering....

When Mary Anne wrote "What an interesting afternoon this turned out to be," she sure was right. I think it was more interesting for me than it was for her, though. Once I got the idea to sculpt Jackie, my mind began working overtime. And my fingers began itching to start the project. I went over to the Rodowskys' the very next afternoon so that I could make some sketches of Jackie to work from, since he couldn't model for me hour after hour. Also, I wanted to ask Mrs. Rodowsky for permission to do the sculpture, and of course I had to ask Jackie himself whether he was interested in being my model.

Boy, was I surprised when I rang the Rodowskys' bell and Mary Anne answered the door! For some reason, I just hadn't expected another club member to be there. I don't know why.

"Claudia!" exclaimed Mary Anne when she saw me on the stoop. The faintest of frowns flickered across her forehead.

"Oh . . ." I said. I was almost speechless. "Um, hi."

"Are you supposed to be sitting?" Mary Anne asked, looking confused.

"Oh, no," I replied. I held out my sketch pad. "I wanted to sketch Jackie. I mean, I want to sculpt him, but I have to sketch him first. Oh, and I have to ask if he can do it."

"We-ell," said Mary Anne slowly. "Mrs. Rodowsky isn't here, of course, but why don't you ask Jackie? *He's* here." Mary Anne sounded a little frazzled.

"Is it one of his bad days?" I asked.

"You could say so. He didn't *mean* to exactly, but he knocked over a ten-pound bag of dog chow, and then got nail polish all over a pair of socks."

"Gosh, what is it with socks, anyway?" I wondered out loud.

"What?"

"Never mind. It's a long story. How did he get nail polish on his socks?"

"That's a long story, too. Why don't you come on in?"

I stepped inside and was greeted by an excited Jackie. "Hi!" he exclaimed. "I'm the only kid here today. Shea's at his piano lesson and Archie's at his tumbling class."

"Don't you like to take lessons?" I asked Jackie.

"Yeah, but I break too many things. Mrs. Schiavone said so."

"Who's Mrs. Schiavone?" Mary Anne and I asked at the same time. We glanced at each other and I could tell she was debating whether to hook my pinkie and say "jinx." I knew because I was wondering the same thing. But we didn't do it.

"Mrs. Schiavone's the piano teacher," Jackie replied. "She lets Shea come to her house because he didn't break her metronome. Or her umbrella. Or her doorbell."

"How did you break her doorbell?" Mary Anne wanted to know.

Jackie frowned. "I'm not sure. But it's broken all right. It used to play 'Somewhere Over the Rainbow.' Now it just goes 'boing, boing, bonk.' "

I tried hard not to giggle. Jackie wasn't laughing and he gets upset about his accidents sometimes — because they really are just accidents. Mary Anne hid her smile, too.

"Jackie," Mary Anne said when the laughing danger was past, "Claudia came over because she wants to ask you something."

"What?" replied Jackie.

He plopped down on the couch and I sat next to him. I explained about the sculpture and the sketches and the art show.

"You want to make a statue of *me?!*" he exclaimed finally.

I couldn't even look at Mary Anne then.

"Well, yes. Sort of. Except that I'm not going to sculpt all of you. Just your head."

"Sculpt my head?" he repeated. "Will it hurt?"

"Not a bit. I won't even touch you."

"And I'll be in a show? Where everyone will see me?"

"Yup."

"Oh, boy! Oh, boy!" was all Jackie could say.

"Do you want to start now?" I asked him. "I need to make some drawings of you."

"Is it okay?" Jackie asked Mary Anne.

"Fine with me," she replied.

I posed Jackie at one end of the couch, settled myself at the other, and began sketching. At first, Jackie sat almost motionlessly. He didn't smile, didn't even blink his eyes.

"Jack-o, you can relax a little," I told him. "You can even move around if you want. I mean, don't stand up, but — "

"How about if I get him a coloring book?" suggested Mary Anne.

"Oh, great," I replied.

While Jackie was coloring and I was sketching, Mary Anne sat in an easy chair. At first she just watched. Then, after what seemed like a very long time, she said, "So, um, how's Ashley?"

110

I shrugged. "Okay, I guess."

Mary Anne gathered up her courage to ask me an important question. I can always tell when she's doing that. Gathering her courage, I mean. She starts to fidget, then she starts breathing heavily, then she's silent for a few moments, and finally she clears her throat. "Ahem."

"Yes?" I replied.

"Claudia, I was wondering. Is Ashley your, um, best friend now?"

"She most certainly is not."

"She isn't?"

"No way."

"But I thought — "

"I thought we were friends, too," I interrupted her. "I thought nobody understood me the way Ashley did, but I guess I was wrong." I paused. "You know what I was wishing yesterday? I was wishing I could talk to Stacey. Stacey — and the rest of you guys — understand me in *other* ways. Ways that mean nothing to Ashley. But Stacey's probably mad at me, too."

"Too?"

"Yeah." I didn't say anything else. I didn't feel like telling Mary Anne about the fight with Ashley just then.

"Claudia?" Jackie spoke up. "You and that

girl who wears the long dresses are mad at each other, aren't you?"

"I guess so," I replied. I flipped a sheet of paper to the back of my pad and started a new drawing.

"Mommy says when you're mad, you have to tell the other person why. Did you do that?"

"I tried to."

"You know what happens when you do?"

"What?"

"Then the other person tells you why he's mad, then you say something, then he says something, and *then* . . ."

"Yes?" I prompted him.

"I don't know. It's funny, but sometimes you're mad all over again."

I smiled at Jackie and he shrugged.

The doorbell rang then. For the first time I noticed that it sounded like *boing, boing, bonk.*

"Hey, did you break this one, too?" I asked Jackie as Mary Anne got up to answer the bell.

"Sort of," he replied sheepishly.

A few seconds later, Mary Anne, wearing a huge, fierce frown, returned. Ashley was right behind her. Mary Anne didn't utter one word. She just stood aside, folded her arms, and looked from Ashley to me as if to say, "Well? What's going on?"

112

"Ashley!" I cried. "What are you doing here?"

Ashley leaned over to look at the sketch I was working on. "I saw your bike outside. What are *you* doing here? I couldn't believe you were baby-sitting again . . . and I see you aren't."

"Nope. I'm starting my sculpture for the show. That should make you happy."

"Not if you're going to sculpt *him*," replied Ashley, pointing.

Jackie's eager face fell.

"*Him* has a name," I told her. "He's Jackie. And he's one of my good friends."

Jackie's smile returned cautiously.

"So you lost your nerve," Ashley went on, as if she hadn't heard me. "You're going to sculpt a person."

"Right."

"Why?"

"Because I'll sculpt what I want to sculpt. I'll sculpt what I do best, and I do people best, even though I still have a lot to learn."

"I'll say. Well, you're not going to learn it from me," retorted Ashley, and she headed for the front door. Her parting words were, "You're ruining your career, you know." Then she let herself out.

"Whoa," said Mary Anne under her breath. "Intense."

Jackie was looking at me worriedly. "It's okay," I told him. "Really."

"Are you still going to put my head in the show?" he asked.

"You bet. That is, if I finish on time."

"Hey, Claud, you know you really stood up to her," said Mary Anne, looking impressed.

"I guess. I mean, I know. But I don't think it did any good. She still doesn't understand what I'm saying."

"She doesn't *want* to understand," Mary Anne corrected me. "And that's a big difference. She knows you don't agree with her."

I nodded thoughtfully.

"Are we going to see you at the next club meeting?" Mary Anne asked carefully.

"I think so. Not today's, because I'm behind in my homework and I got a D on a spelling test. And there's this library project I haven't even begun yet. So I'm going to hit the books."

"But couldn't you come back from the library by five-thirty?"

"Usually, but . . . just not this time." The problem was, I didn't think I'd be welcome at the meeting. Even if it was in my own room.

"All right," said Mary Anne briskly. "I'll tell the others."

114

"Okay." I gathered up my pencils and closed the pad. "I've got enough sketches for now, Jack-o," I told him. "Thanks a lot."

It was time to go. I had a lot to do. And I mean a *lot*.

CHAPTER 13

One of the best things to do when you have a *lot* to do, is make a list. Then you can cross things off as you complete them. Also, you won't forget anything. After dinner that evening, the first thing I did was go to my room and make a list of lists to make. That's how behind I was!

This is what my first list looked like:

<u>List of Lists of Things to Do</u>
1. Freinds
2. Schoolwork
3. Scupture ~~show~~ show

This is what my second list looked like:

<u>Things to Do: Freinds</u>
1. Call Ashley -- try to explian
2. Call Stacey -- aplogise

3. Call Kristy -- apologise. Tell her will try to be at neat meeting

This is what my third list looked like:

School Work To do
1. Ask Mrs. Hall if I can take speling test agian
2. GO TO THE LIBRARY AGAIN !!! Work on projext abot War of 1812.
3. Finish _the 21 Ballons_
4. Start _A Wrinkel in Time_

This is what my last list looked like:

Thing to Do: Scupture Show
1. Think very carfuly aboat how much time I need for new sclupture.
2. Talk to Ms. Bear?
3. Talk to Mom and dad?

I sat on my bed and looked at all my lists. Then I threw away the first one since I'd made the other three lists. I felt very organized — and very panicked. How could I get everything done?

I didn't know, but the best thing to do was dig right in. The number-one item on the Friends list was to call Ashley. So I did. I closed the door to my room, curled up on my bed, and dialed her number. I'd called her a lot lately, so I knew her number by heart.

"Hi, Ashley," I said, after Mrs. Wyeth had called her to the phone. "It's me."

"Who?"

"*Me*. Claudia."

"Oh."

"Well, it's nice to talk to you, too," I said sarcastically.

"Look, I'm really busy — " Ashley began.

"Tell me about it," I replied, glancing nervously at my lists. "Listen, I'm calling because I have to tell you something. I want you to try to understand this."

"What?"

"That my life is very . . . big. I mean, there's a lot to it. I have friends and my family and school and art and pottery and baby-sitting. Maybe someday I'll decide I want to narrow things down, but not right now. I like to try new things. I like, what do you call it? Variety, I guess. I'm happiest when I'm busy, even if sometimes I'm too busy.

"I really like you, Ashley, but I can't spend all my time with you, working on sculptures, even if you are the most talented person I know. Do you see what I mean?"

118

"Yes," replied Ashley after a pause, "I do."

And then she hung up on me.

For a moment I sat and stared at the receiver. I wanted to cry. Ashley didn't like me anymore. She probably didn't value me as an artist anymore, either. But what had I really lost? Certainly not a friend. A real friend would have listened and tried to understand. A real friend would not have hung up on me. Ashley was not a real friend. It wasn't that she was a mean person or a bad person; it was that art was the only thing that truly mattered to her. So if I wasn't going to be as serious an artist as Ashley, then I didn't much matter to her. Ashley's only friend was art.

I hoped my theory about a real friend not hanging up on me was true — because I was about to call Stacey. If she hung up on me, I'd be crushed. But I dialed her number anyway. I'd just crossed item number one off list number two and I had to move on to item number two.

Stacey answered the phone before the first ring was finished. She must have been sitting on her bed. (She has a phone extension in her bedroom, but not a private, personal phone number like I do.)

"Hi, Stace," I said tentatively.

"Claudia?"

"Yeah, it's me. Stacey, I'm calling to apologize. I know I've been a really rotten friend. I got all carried away with Ashley because she studied at the Keyes Art Society and said I had talent." For five more minutes I explained everything to Stacey. When I finished, she was still on the other end of the phone.

"Claudia," she said, and she sounded as if she were trying not to laugh. "Reach under your pillow."

"My pillow? Okay." I felt underneath it and my fingers closed over a wadded-up piece of paper.

"Did you find the note?" she asked.

"Yeah."

"Then read it, ignore it, and throw it away."

The note said: In my breadbox of friends, you are a CRUMB.

It was kind of funny, but I didn't laugh. I threw it away as Stacey had instructed.

"Did you write that?" I asked.

"Yes. But I only meant it a little. Claud, we're still friends. At least, I still want to be your friend. But I think we have some things to talk about."

"I agree," I told her.

We decided to try to find a time to talk in

person. Maybe in school or before the next meeting.

I crossed item number two off list number two and phoned Kristy.

Karen, Kristy's little stepsister, answered the phone. "Claudia!" she exclaimed. "We're having a terrible night over here! Ben Brewer's ghost hypnotized Boo-Boo, and — "

"Karen," I interrupted, "I'm really sorry, but I have to talk to Kristy. Can you get her for me, please?"

Karen grew all huffy, but she brought Kristy to the phone. When Kristy was on, I started my little speech all over again. Then I told her that I was probably going to spend my lunch periods in the Resource Room making up work, but that I would definitely be at the next club meeting.

"Okay," said Kristy shortly. "Great." She sounded as if she didn't believe me.

"I really will be there."

"Fine."

"I'll even call Dawn and tell her she can go back to being the alternate officer again."

"Okay."

"Okay."

"'Bye."

"'Bye."

That wasn't much of a start, but it was something. I'd just have to be patient, and I certainly better turn up at the meeting.

I spent the rest of the evening and a lot of that weekend doing homework and looking at the sketches I'd made of Jackie. By the time I went to bed on Sunday, I'd reached an important decision.

"Ms. Baehr?"

"Yes, Claudia?"

Another art class was over. Ashley had sat in the front of the room. I'd sat in the back. With the sketches of Jackie spread across the table, I'd begun my sculpture. Now, the rest of the students were gone. I'd just called Ms. Baehr over to look at my work.

"I like the subject you finally chose," she said, smiling approvingly.

"Me, too," I replied. "But I'm not going to be able to finish this in time for the show. I've only got one more week. I have schoolwork to catch up on — you know how my parents feel about that — and other things to do, too. So I'm not going to enter anything in the show. I'll talk to Mom and Dad tonight. I'll work on this sculpture for class, but it won't be ready for the show."

"Claudia, I wish you'd re-think this," replied Ms. Baehr. "If you work hard, I think you *could* finish in time."

"Only if I drop everything else, and I don't want to do that."

Ms. Baehr nodded. "All right. I respect your decision."

"Thanks," I said. "Thanks a lot."

I did talk to my parents that night. They were surprised that I'd decided not to be in the show, but they have this thing about school. They think it is very, *very*, VERY important. So when they heard that I was putting school before art, they were delighted. Even though they tried not to show it.

After I was finished talking with my parents I went to my room, settled myself at my desk, and looked over the lists I'd made the night before. I'd done everything on the Friends list so I threw it away. I'd done everything on the Sculpture Show list so I threw that away, too. My School Work list was not in such good shape, which wasn't surprising. Hardly anything having to do with schoolwork is in good shape if I'm involved.

However, I had asked Mrs. Hall if I could take the spelling test again — and she'd said yes! I reached into my pencil jar so I could cross off item number one. I pulled out a pencil with a piece of paper wrapped around it.

I sighed. Another note.

I unrolled the paper. The note was in Kristy's handwriting. It said: Famous jerks — Benedict Arnold, the Wicked Witch of the West, Claudia Kishi.

I threw away the note and crossed off number one on the list. I couldn't cross off two, three, or four, though. But that was all right. Soon I'd be able to. I was almost finished with *The Twenty-One Balloons* and I'd taken *A Wrinkle in Time* by Madeleine L'Engle out of the library. While I was thinking about it, I opened *A Wrinkle in Time* and read the first sentence. "It was a dark and stormy night." Well, that didn't sound so bad. In fact, it sounded kind of like the Nancy Drew books I like so much. And the titles of the first three chapters were "Mrs. Whatsit," "Mrs. Who," and "Mrs. Which." They sounded like fun! I looked longingly at the book as I put it aside to start studying for my spelling test. Maybe finishing up my School Work list would go quickly after all. I smiled.

And tomorrow I would go to a meeting of the Baby-sitters Club.

CHAPTER 14

The next day, I packed a lunch (something I hardly ever do) and at lunchtime went to the Resource Room. I'd done that the last couple of days, too. This time, I brought *The Twenty-One Balloons* with me. I had finished reading it, and now I needed someone to quiz me on the spelling of the hard words so I could get ready to retake the spelling test. One of the Resource Room teachers worked hard with me during the whole lunch period. I was proud of myself. Maybe I wouldn't get an A on the test, but I thought I could get a C or even a B.

After school, I had to do a chore. Well, maybe chore isn't the right word, but I *had* to do something I didn't *want* to do. That certainly sounded like a chore.

As soon as I got home, I jumped on my bike and rode over to Jackie Rodowsky's house. The Rodowskys weren't expecting me, so Jackie's mother was a little surprised to see me standing on the front stoop.

"Claudia!" she said. "Has there been a mix-up? Did I — "

"Oh, no," I interrupted. "I came to talk to Jackie. Is he home from school yet?"

"He got here a few minutes ago. Come on in, honey."

Mrs. Rodowsky led me inside just as Jackie came bounding downstairs, leaped over the last three, stumbled against a table as he landed, and knocked a vase to the floor. Luckily, it landed on the rug and didn't break.

"Whoops," said Jackie.

Mrs. Rodowsky shook her head. But all she said was, "Jackie, Claudia's here to see you." Then she disappeared into the kitchen.

"Claudia!" Jackie exclaimed. "Are you going to start sculpting my head?"

"Not today," I replied. "That's what I wanted to talk to you about. Come sit with me." I sat down on a sofa and patted the cushion next to me.

Jackie charged across the room and threw himself down on the couch, accidentally kicking my right knee.

"Ow!" I couldn't help crying out.

"Oops. Sorry."

"Jackie," I began, rubbing my knee, "I came

126

over to tell you something. I'm really sorry, but I'm not going to be able to put you in the show after all."

Jackie had been bouncing and wiggling around. Now he stopped. "You're *not?*" he said. His eyes began to fill with tears.

"No," I replied. As simply as I could, I explained how I'd run out of time.

Jackie didn't say anything. He poked the end of his shoelace inside his sock.

"I'd still like to sculpt you, though," I told him.

"You would?"

"Yup. I showed the drawings of you to my teacher and she really liked them. She wants me to sculpt you, too."

"But no show?"

"No show. . . . Would you like to be my model anyway?"

Jackie screwed up his face in thought. "Yes," he replied at last.

"Great!" I said. "I'm sure you're going to be a terrific model. I am sorry about the show, but I wanted you to know the truth if I was going to sculpt you."

Jackie nodded. "You know what, Claudia?"

"What?"

"I love you." Jackie wrapped his arms around my waist and I hugged him back.

I was glad I'd been honest with him. A smile spread across my face as I realized something. I hadn't been baby-sitting much lately and I *missed* little kids. Only someone Jackie's age would hug me and thank me when I'd just disappointed him.

When I left the Rodowskys' I rode over to the public library. I worked on my War of 1812 project again. But when the clock over the front door said 5:10, I gathered up my papers and notebook, hopped on my bike, and rode home. I reached my house at 5:31 and ran to my room. Kristy, Mary Anne, Dawn, and Stacey were already there.

"Hi, everybody!" I exclaimed. "I'm back!"

I flopped onto the floor and looked around. Kristy was sitting in the director's chair, drinking a soda and wearing her visor. Mary Anne and Dawn were lying across my bed on their backs. Stacey was perched on my desk.

"Hi," the others replied. They didn't look at me.

"Any calls yet?" I asked.

"Nope."

"Good. Then it's time for . . ." I reached under my bed and pulled out a Hershey's Kisses bag, only I knew there weren't any Hershey's Kisses in it. I held the bag out. "Everyone has to take one, even you, Stacey."

"But I can't — " she began.

I held up my hand for silence. Then I offered the bag to Kristy. She reached in and pulled out a folded piece of paper. Everyone else did the same.

"Now," I said, "who has the paper with the number one on it?"

"I do," said Dawn, unfolding the note.

"Okay, you read yours first. Then whoever has number two, read yours. And then three and then four, okay? Dawn?"

Dawn cleared her throat. " 'Friends,' " she announced, reading the title. " 'Long ago in another time, I had four friends and they were mine.' " Dawn stopped and looked around.

"Oh," said Stacey. "Um, 'Then I found an artist who, said I am good and so are you.' "

" 'So I followed her here and there,' " read Kristy, " 'and round and round and everywhere.' " She giggled.

" 'But,' " went on Mary Anne, " 'she was false and it took you, to show me friends that are really true.' "

When Mary Anne was finished, no one said anything.

"I guess," I spoke up, "that's my way of saying I'm sorry. And that I kind of learned the hard way who my real friends are. I, um, really missed you guys. And baby-sitting. And meetings. And I'm sick to death of animated objects or whatever they're called. I know you're still mad, but I hope we can be friends again. Someday."

"Oh, that is so sad and lovely!" cried Mary Anne and burst into tears.

At *that*, Kristy burst out *laughing*.

"Lunatics," said Stacey. "We have a club full of fools."

"Club of fools!" I repeated, and then everyone laughed, even Mary Anne.

"I'm not asking you guys to forgive me right now," I went on. "I know it'll take time — "

"Claudia, Claudia, Claudia," said Stacey. "Save your breath. We forgive you."

"You do?" I asked.

"We do?" Kristy asked.

"Yes," said Stacey firmly, glaring at Kristy, "*we do*."

I began to feel teary-eyed myself then. "I don't deserve friends as good as you," I choked out. "I'm too lucky."

"Oh, Claudia!" wailed Stacey. She slid off the desk and ran over to me and we hugged.

"Hey, are you wearing new perfume?" I asked her, sniffing.

"Yeah!" she exclaimed. "Do you like it? It's called Moonlight Mist."

"It's fabulous."

"Let me smell," said the others, crowding in.

"Ooh, nice," breathed Dawn.

"Heavenly," added Mary Anne.

"It's okay — if you want to smell like a rosebed," said Kristy.

We were all talking at the same time.

"What's wrong with a rosebed?" Mary Anne wanted to know.

"Can I try some?" I asked.

"Sure, I've got the bottle right here in — "

Ring, ring.

The phone!

"Oh, can I get it? Puh-*lease?* It feels like years since I've taken a job call," I exclaimed.

"Go to it," replied Kristy.

"Hello, Baby-sitters Club," I said, picking up the receiver. "Yes. . . . Yes. . . . Oh, no problem. . . . Sure. Okay, call you right back. 'Bye." I hung up the phone and faced the others. Mary Anne was holding the record book in her lap, pencil poised.

"Who was it?" asked Kristy.

"Mrs. Newton. She needs a sitter for Jamie and Lucy next Thursday evening. It won't be a late night. They'll be back by nine."

"Let's see," said Mary Anne. "You're free then, Claud. Want the job?"

"Sure!" I replied. I called Mrs. Newton back

to give her the information. As I was talking, I began to feel like a real, official club member again. "Boy," I said when I'd hung up. "It sure is good to be back with you guys."

"Claudia?" asked Mary Anne seriously from the spot on my bed. "What happened?"

"What happened?" I repeated. "What do you mean?"

"I mean with Ashley and the club and us."

"Oh. That. . . . I just got carried away, I guess. You have to understand something. Hardly anybody ever tells me I'm *really* good at something. I mean, actually *talented*. When you're me, that just doesn't happen often."

"We always say how good you are in art," Mary Anne pointed out, looking hurt.

"I know. And that means a lot. But the thing is, if you'll excuse me for saying this, you guys don't know much about art. So your comments are nice but . . . when Ashley came along, and she *was* an excellent artist and she had even studied at Keyes, well, her comments meant a *lot*. Suddenly I felt very important. At least I did when I was with her. And I didn't want to lose that."

Mary Anne and Stacey were nodding slowly.

"I see," said Stacey. "I understand."

"But it turned out that Ashley only liked my talent," I went on. "I mean, she liked the person she *thought* I was, and she doesn't really want to hang around anyone who isn't an artist. But that's not what makes a friendship, is it? I mean, if *we* didn't like baby-sitting, we would still be friends."

"Right," said Stacey.

"Right," said Dawn, Kristy, and Mary Anne.

"And now," added Kristy, "let's get down to business. Where's the treasury? We have money to count, dues to be paid."

We all got to work.

And I thought, I'm back, I'm really back!

CHAPTER 15

"Oh, I am so nervous. I am so nervous!" I kept exclaiming.

"Relax, Claud, you're going to give yourself apoplexy," said Kristy.

I was even too nervous to ask Kristy what apoplexy was.

It was 7:45 in the evening. Milling around in front of Stoneybrook's new art gallery were a bunch of students from the Arts Center and their families and friends. I was there with Mom, Dad, Mimi, my sister Janine, and the members of the Baby-sitters Club.

In exactly fifteen minutes, the front door was going to open and everyone would be allowed inside to see the new gallery — and the Arts Center sculpture show. I wasn't nervous about the opening of the gallery. That was exciting, but it wasn't enough to give me appendicitis, or whatever Kristy had said. No, I was nervous because of a phone call I'd gotten that afternoon. I'd picked up the receiver, and Ms. Baehr had been on the other end of the line.

"Claudia?" she'd said.

"Yes?" I'd replied, trying to get over my shock. (You just never expect a teacher to call you at home.)

"I have to tell you something. I'm not sure I should have done this, but I did, so it's too late." She paused. "I entered your sculpture of Jackie in the art show."

"You what?!" I cried. "But it isn't finished! It's, maybe, half-finished."

"I know. I entered it as a work-in-progress. It's wonderful, Claudia. I want people to see it. . . . Claudia?"

"I'm still here. I — don't know what to say."

"Don't say anything. Just come to the show tonight. Bring your family. By the time the gallery opens, the prizes will have been awarded."

So you can see why I was nervous. I didn't think I'd won an award. Not for a work-in-progress. But that half-finished piece was going to be on display. And I didn't want anyone laughing at it.

Oh, I thought now, I should never have mentioned the show to my friends. Why had I done that? (Maybe because I'd still been in shock.) Of course they'd wanted to come — Mary Anne had even brought her father — and now they'd be around to see the laughers.

A new worry came to me. Ashley would be there and she'd see the laughers, too, only she'd probably join them.

I shook my head. What a mess.

A murmur in the crowd made me stop worrying. The front door was opening. People were streaming inside.

My heart began to beat as loudly as a train running down a track. I could feel it pumping in my throat.

"I think I'm going to faint," I said to Stacey.

"Oh, Claud, you are not," she replied. Nevertheless, she reached out her hand and I grabbed it. We entered the exhibit like two little kids on their first day of kindergarten.

My family, my friends, and I stood in a group and looked around. The new art gallery was lovely. It was all carpeted and quiet, and everything was gray or white — so as not to distract from the art that was on display. Usually, I guessed, paintings would be hung on the movable partitions that divided the gallery into rooms, but now our sculptures stood proudly on brown pedestals. I could see about twenty in the room we had entered. The rest must be in other rooms. Ms. Baehr had said about sixty pieces were on display.

Still gripping hands, Stacey and I began walking from sculpture to sculpture. Some of them were hard to see because of the crowd, but we waited patiently or stood on tiptoe until we could get a glimpse of each one. I was determined not to miss a thing.

"Look! There's something by Mary Drabek!" exclaimed Dawn. "She's in my math class."

"Hey, she got a third-prize ribbon!" said Kristy, wiggling her way closer to the sculpture.

"This is very impressive, honey," my mother said to me. "I think the new gallery is wonderful. You should be proud to be in its first exhibit."

I nodded my head. I was afraid to speak. Where was my sculpture of Jackie? I didn't hear any laughing. . . .

Stacey and I had finally dropped hands. Soon I got separated from my family and the club members, so I wandered around by myself. I made a complete tour of the first room and didn't find Jackie.

I entered the next room.

The first piece I saw was a boxing cow by John Steiner. It hadn't won an award.

The next piece was Fiona MacRae's. It was the stag she'd been working on. The second-prize ribbon was attached to it.

I passed a rabbit, two little girls holding hands, a man reading a newspaper, and a baseball player.

And then I reached a small crowd of people. They weren't laughing so they couldn't have been looking at Jackie. I edged closer, squeezing between a man who smelled of tobacco and a woman with a baby in a Snuggli. There on a brown pedestal was Ashley's fireplug. The blue first-prize ribbon hung jauntily in front of it.

I was amazed. Somehow, Ashley really had managed to make that hydrant come to life. And the judges must have appreciated what she'd done.

"It's an animated inanimate object," I heard a voice explain.

Ashley.

There she was.

Our eyes met.

I smiled. "Congratulations," I mouthed to her.

Ashley nodded at me and then smiled back.

I left the room. Suddenly, I wasn't very interested in finding my sculpture. I didn't care where it was or whether anyone was laughing at it. Maybe I should have listened to Ashley more. Maybe I really could have learned from her.

But just at that moment, I heard an excited squeal behind me.

"Claudia!" Kristy cried. She had grabbed my arm and was jumping up and down. "Come see what I found!"

Kristy led me into a third room. Then she picked up her pace and pulled me straight through it, nearly knocking a bunch of people over.

"What *is* it?" I exclaimed, half-annoyed, half-amused.

"It's . . . this sculpture!"

In front of me was Jackie. Kristy had been the first of us to find it. Right away, I noticed two things: no one was laughing at it, and a green ribbon had been fixed to the pedestal.

"You got an honorable mention!" said Kristy.

"For a work-in-progress," I marveled.

"You would have won first prize if you'd finished," someone spoke up behind me.

It was Ms. Baehr.

"I would have?"

She nodded. "The judges were very impressed."

"You'll have to tell Jackie," said Kristy.

"I'll say."

The next half hour was one of the most exciting I've ever known. My parents and sister and Mimi and Mary Anne and her dad and Dawn and Stacey all crowded around to look at and exclaim over the half-finished sculpture of Jackie. Then a *Stoneybrook News* photographer took a picture of all the winners, even the three of us who just got honorable mentions. She said that the photo and an article about us and the gallery would appear in the paper a few days later.

All that night people kept congratulating me. Even my sister, who wants to be a physicist and whose head is usually in the clouds, said, "This must be most rewarding for you. You're among very talented company." And Mimi hugged me to her and said, "I love you, my Claudia."

The next day I was sitting with my friends in the cafeteria. We were back to our regular old lunch routine. Kristy and Mary Anne had bought the hot lunch, Dawn had brought a health food lunch from home, and Stacey and I had bought sandwiches.

Kristy was saying, "You know the smell of sneakers after gym class? And you know the smell of Cuthbert Athlete's Foot Creme? Well, if you mixed those smells together, wouldn't they smell just like this pot roast?" and Mary

Anne was practically gagging, when I glanced up and saw Ashley walk by our table with her tray. She was alone as usual, looking for a place to sit.

I'm not sure what got into me, but I jumped up and ran to her. I touched her arm. "Ashley?"

"Yes?" she replied, turning around. "Oh . . . Claudia."

"Um, I was wondering. Do you have someplace to sit? I mean, would you like to sit with my friends and me?"

"With you?" Ashley glanced at the members of the Baby-sitters Club who were, of course, watching us curiously. "Well . . ."

"Oh, come on," I said. I knew perfectly well that Ashley and I would never be best friends. And I knew she would never understand my interest in baby-sitting. *I* would never understand how she could think *only* of art. But we did have things in common. I felt that we could be friendly. I wanted to give it a try, at least.

I pulled Ashley over to our table. "Go ahead. Sit down," I said.

Ashley did, somewhat reluctantly.

Kristy scowled at me, and I knew why. Ashley looked just plain weird in her outfit — a long knitted vest over an even longer shirt which she was wearing tails-out over a skirt that didn't match either the vest or the skirt. And there were those hiking boots again.

But the first thing Ashley did when she sat down was sniff at her lunch and say, "You know what this meat smells like?"

"Old sneakers and athlete's foot creme?" suggested Kristy.

"Well, I was going to say turpentine, rubber cement, and acrylic paint," replied Ashley. "I guess that's pretty much the same."

Kristy grinned. "Yeah, I guess so."

And then we began to laugh. All of us. Afterward, Ashley and I got into a discussion about sculpture, and my friends listened. Then my friends and I got into a discussion about baby-sitting for kids who don't like baby-sitters, and Ashley listened.

When lunch was over, we left the cafeteria together.

After that day, Ashley sometimes sat with us but often sat alone. Either way, it was okay. She and I had become sometimes friends, and that was okay, too. Like Jackie Rodowsky's accidents, those things just happened —sometimes.

Dear Reader,

In *Claudia and the New Girl*, we get our first close look at Claudia's passion for art. When I was growing up, art was a very important part of my life. I took after-school art classes starting when I was five. From kindergarten through high school, I thoroughly enjoyed art, and looked forward to any class I was taking. And I was very lucky to have a lot of good art teachers. Like Claudia, I enjoyed all aspects of art — painting and drawing, sculpting, making mosaics, and jewelry-making.

As an adult, I still enjoy creative activities, my favorites being sewing and needlework, like Mary Anne. One reason I enjoy both writing and art is that I find they are great ways to express yourself.

Happy reading and drawing,

Ann M Martin

L. GODWIN

Ann M. Martin

About the Author

ANN MATTHEWS MARTIN was born on August 12, 1955. She grew up in Princeton, NJ, with her parents and her younger sister, Jane.

Although Ann used to be a teacher and then an editor of children's books, she's now a full-time writer. She gets the ideas for her books from many different places. Some are based on personal experiences. Others are based on childhood memories and feelings. Many are written about contemporary problems or events.

All of Ann's characters, even the members of the Baby-sitters Club, are made up. (So is Stoneybrook.) But many of her characters are based on real people. Sometimes Ann names her characters after people she knows, other times she chooses names she likes.

In addition to the Baby-sitters Club books, Ann Martin has written many other books for children. Her favorite is *Ten Kids, No Pets* because she loves big families and she loves animals. Her favorite Baby-sitters Club book is *Kristy's Big Day*. (By the way, Kristy is her favorite baby-sitter!)

Ann M. Martin now lives in New York with her cats, Gussie and Woody. Her hobbies are reading, sewing, and needlework — especially making clothes for children.

Notebook Pages

This Baby-sitters Club book belongs to _____ .

I am _____ years old and in the _____ grade.

The name of my school is _____ .

I got this BSC book from _____ .

I started reading it on _____ and

finished reading it on _____ .

The place where I read most of this book is _____ .

My favorite part was when _____

If I could change anything in the story, it might be the part when

_____ .

My favorite character in the Baby-sitters Club is _____ .

The BSC member I am most like is _____

because _____ .

If I could write a Baby-sitters Club book it would be about _____

_____

_____

#12 Claudia and the New Girl

Claudia loves to draw almost more than anything. One of my favorite things to do is _____. I like it because _____ _____. One thing that I'd really like to start doing is _____. I want to do this because _____ _____.

Claudia gets really excited about sculpting Jackie Rodowsky for her art competition. If I could paint or sculpt anything/anyone, I would choose _____ _____. I would choose this subject because ___ _____.

Claudia isn't crazy about school — except for art class. My favorite class is _____ because _____ _____.

My least favorite class is _____ because _____ _____.

Even though art is really important to Claudia, she has lots of other important things in her life. The most important things in my life are _____.

CLAUDIA'S

Finger painting at 3...

A spooky sitting adventu

*Sitting for two of my favorite charges --
Jamie and Lucy Newton.*

SCRAPBOOK

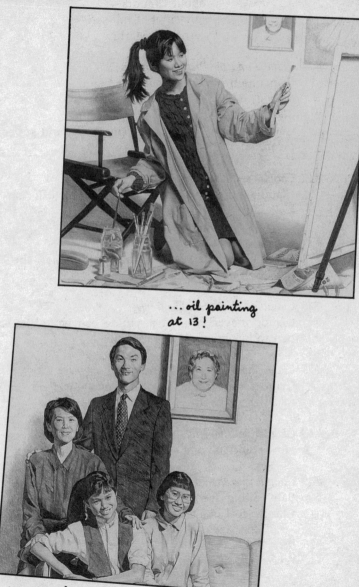

...oil painting
at 13!

my family. Mom and Dad, me and
Janine... and we'll never forget Mimi.

Interior art by Angelo Tillery

Read all the books
about **Claudia**
in the Baby-sitters Club series
by Ann M. Martin

THE BABY-SITTERS CLUB®

by Ann M. Martin

More titles... ➡

The Baby-sitters Club titles continued...

❑ MG47011-6	#73 Mary Anne and Miss Priss	$3.50
❑ MG47012-4	#74 Kristy and the Copycat	$3.50
❑ MG47013-2	#75 Jessi's Horrible Prank	$3.50
❑ MG47014-0	#76 Stacey's Lie	$3.50
❑ MG48221-1	#77 Dawn and Whitney, Friends Forever	$3.50
❑ MG48222-X	#78 Claudia and Crazy Peaches	$3.50
❑ MG48223-8	#79 Mary Anne Breaks the Rules	$3.50
❑ MG48224-6	#80 Mallory Pike, #1 Fan	$3.50
❑ MG48225-4	#81 Kristy and Mr. Mom	$3.50
❑ MG48226-2	#82 Jessi and the Troublemaker	$3.50
❑ MG48235-1	#83 Stacey vs. the BSC	$3.50
❑ MG48228-9	#84 Dawn and the School Spirit War	$3.50
❑ MG48236-X	#85 Claudi Kishi, Live from WSTO	$3.50
❑ MG48227-0	#86 Mary Anne and Camp BSC	$3.50
❑ MG48237-8	#87 Stacey and the Bad Girls	$3.50
❑ MG22872-2	#88 Farewell, Dawn	$3.50
❑ MG22873-0	#89 Kristy and the Dirty Diapers	$3.50
❑ MG45575-3	Logan's Story Special Edition Readers' Request	$3.25
❑ MG47118-X	Logan Bruno, Boy Baby-sitter Special Edition Readers' Request	$3.50
❑ MG47756-0	Shannon's Story Special Edition	$3.50
❑ MG44240-6	Baby-sitters on Board! Super Special #1	$3.95
❑ MG44239-2	Baby-sitters' Summer Vacation Super Special #2	$3.95
❑ MG43973-1	Baby-sitters' Winter Vacation Super Special #3	$3.95
❑ MG42493-9	Baby-sitters' Island Adventure Super Special #4	$3.95
❑ MG43575-2	California Girls! Super Special #5	$3.95
❑ MG43576-0	New York, New York! Super Special #6	$3.95
❑ MG44963-X	Snowbound Super Special #7	$3.95
❑ MG44962-X	Baby-sitters at Shadow Lake Super Special #8	$3.95
❑ MG45661-X	Starring the Baby-sitters Club Super Special #9	$3.95
❑ MG45674-1	Sea City, Here We Come! Super Special #10	$3.95
❑ MG47015-9	The Baby-sitter's Remember Super Special #11	$3.95
❑ MG48308-0	Here Come the Bridesmaids Super Special #12	$3.95

Available wherever you buy books...or use this order form.

Scholastic Inc., P.O. Box 7502, 2931 E. McCarty Street, Jefferson City, MO 65102

Please send me the books I have checked above. I am enclosing $ _____ (please add $2.00 to cover shipping and handling). Send check or money order—no cash or C.O.D.s please.

Name _____ Birthdate _____

Address _____

City _____ State/Zip _____

Please allow four to six weeks for delivery. Offer good in the U.S. only. Sorry, mail orders are not available to residents of Canada. Prices subject to change.

BSC395

Now **THE BABY-SITTERS CLUB** ®

★ **is a Video Club too!**

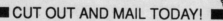